THE THINGS THEY CARRIED

Tim O'Brien

© 2002 by Spark Publishing

All rights reserved. No part of this publication may be reproduced, stored in a retrieval system, or transmitted, in any form or by any means, electronic, mechanical, photocopying, recording, or otherwise, without prior written permission from the publisher.

SPARKNOTES is a registered trademark of SparkNotes LLC.

Spark Publishing
A Division of Barnes & Noble
120 Fifth Avenue
New York, NY 10011
www.sparknotes.com

ISBN-13: 978-1-5866-3827-6
ISBN-10: 1-5866-3827-0

Please submit changes or report errors to www.sparknotes.com/errors.

Printed and bound in the United States

9 10 8

Introduction: Stopping to Buy Sparknotes on a Snowy Evening

Whose words these are you *think* you know.
Your paper's due tomorrow, though;
We're glad to see you stopping here
To get some help before you go.

Lost your course? You'll find it here.
Face tests and essays without fear.
Between the words, good grades at stake:
Get great results throughout the year.

Once school bells caused your heart to quake
As teachers circled each mistake.
Use SparkNotes and no longer weep,
Ace every single test you take.

Yes, books are lovely, dark, and deep,
But only what you grasp you keep,
With hours to go before you sleep,
With hours to go before you sleep.

CONTENTS

CONTEXT	1
PLOT OVERVIEW	5
CHARACTER LIST	7
ANALYSIS OF MAJOR CHARACTERS	11
TIM O'BRIEN	11
JIMMY CROSS	12
MITCHELL SANDERS	12
KIOWA	13
THEMES, MOTIFS & SYMBOLS	15
PHYSICAL AND EMOTIONAL BURDENS	15
FEAR OF SHAME AS MOTIVATION	16
THE SUBJECTION OF TRUTH TO STORYTELLING	16
STORYTELLING	17
AMBIGUOUS MORALITY	18
LONELINESS AND ISOLATION	18
THE DEAD YOUNG VIETNAMESE SOLDIER	19
KATHLEEN	20
LINDA	20
SUMMARY & ANALYSIS	21
"THE THINGS THEY CARRIED"	21
"LOVE"	24
"SPIN"	26
"ON THE RAINY RIVER"	28
"ENEMIES" & "FRIENDS"	32
"HOW TO TELL A TRUE WAR STORY"	34
"THE DENTIST"	37
"SWEETHEART OF THE SONG TRA BONG"	38
"STOCKINGS"	41
"CHURCH"	42
"THE MAN I KILLED"	44
"AMBUSH"	47

"STYLE"	48
"SPEAKING OF COURAGE"	50
"NOTES"	52
"IN THE FIELD"	55
"GOOD FORM"	57
"FIELD TRIP"	58
"THE GHOST SOLDIERS"	60
"NIGHT LIFE"	63
"THE LIVES OF THE DEAD"	64
IMPORTANT QUOTATIONS EXPLAINED	67
KEY FACTS	73
STUDY QUESTIONS & ESSAY TOPICS	75
REVIEW & RESOURCES	79
QUIZ	79
SUGGESTIONS FOR FURTHER READING	84

Context

WILLIAM TIMOTHY O'BRIEN WAS BORN on October 1, 1946, to an insurance salesman and an elementary school teacher in Austin, Minnesota. He was raised in Worthington, a small town in southern Minnesota that he would later describe as what one would find if one "look[ed] in a dictionary under the word boring." As a child, the overweight and introspective O'Brien spent his time practicing magic tricks and making pilgrimages to the public library. His father's *New York Times* accounts of fighting in Iwo Jima and Okinawa during World War II inspired O'Brien to consider a career in writing. When O'Brien arrived at Macalester College in St. Paul, Minnesota, he decided to focus his studies on political science. His college years, however, were spent trying to ignore the Vietnam War or railing against it—he attended peace vigils and war protests and aspired to join the State Department. He graduated summa cum laude and Phi Beta Kappa and had already been accepted to a Ph.D. program at Harvard University's School of Government when he received his draft notice, two weeks after graduation.

Faced with the prospect of fighting in the war he so actively opposed, the twenty-two-year-old O'Brien felt pulled between his convictions, which could be kept intact by escaping across the border to Canada, and the expectations of those in his hometown who, he once said, "couldn't spell the word 'Hanoi' if you spotted them three vowels." Though torn, he entered the military for basic training at Fort Lewis, Washington, on August 14, 1968. When he arrived in Vietnam in February 1969, he served in the Fifth Battalion of the 46th Infantry, 198th Infantry Brigade, American Division until March 1970. O'Brien's area of operations was in the Quang Ngai Province, where he later set *The Things They Carried*.

O'Brien's service brought him to the South Vietnamese village of My Lai a year after the infamous massacre of 1968. He was eventually wounded and returned home with a Purple Heart, a Bronze Star for Valor, and a Combat Infantry Badge. He also had a storehouse of guilt and an endless supply of observations and anecdotes that would later comprise his memoir *If I Die in a Combat Zone, Box Me Up and Ship Me Home*. This work was published in 1973 as O'Brien was abandoning his graduate studies for a career as a national affairs reporter for the *Washington Post*. That reporting stint lasted a year. In 1975 he published *Northern Lights*, an account of two brothers in rural Minnesota. *Going After Cacciato*, which won the National Book Award in 1979 over John Irving's *The World According to Garp* and John Cheever's *Stories*, was the account of a platoon forced to chase one of its AWOL soliders. Winning the National Book Award solidified O'Brien's reputation as a masterful writer concerned with the ambiguities of love and war. Following this success came *The Nuclear Age*, a novel about a draft-dodger obsessed with the idea of nuclear holocaust, published in 1985.

After *The Nuclear Age*'s home-front comedy, O'Brien returned his attention to the battlefields. He wrote a short story, "Speaking of Courage," that was originally meant for inclusion in *Going After Cacciato*. In 1990, "Speaking of Courage" was one of twenty-two stories included in *The Things They Carried*, a sequence of lyrical and interrelated stories that has been heralded as one of the finest volumes of fiction about the Vietnam War. The work gained attention and wide acclaim not only for its subject matter but also for its honesty and specificity, its discussion of fact and fiction, and its commentary on memory and on the act of storytelling itself. Much of the material in the work has been drawn from O'Brien's experiences; he felt so close to his stories that he dedicated the work to his characters—Jimmy Cross, Norman Bowker, Rat Kiley, Mitchell Sanders, Henry Dobbins, and Kiowa. The most striking elimination of the boundary between fact and fiction is the narrator and protagonist's name, Tim O'Brien. The main character also has grown up in Worthington, Minnesota, and has attended Macalester College. Like the real O'Brien, the fictional O'Brien becomes a writer who records many of his Vietnam experiences in stories and novels. Nevertheless, several discrepancies exist between the two men. Unlike his protagonist, for example, the real O'Brien never killed a man while at war, and he doesn't have any children.

The Things They Carried was a finalist for both the Pulitzer Prize and the National Book Critics Circle Award, and it earned O'Brien comparisons to several eminent fiction writers. Two to whom he is often connected are Stephen Crane and Kurt Vonnegut. Crane's *The Red Badge of Courage*, published in 1895, follows a Union regiment during the Civil War and specifically concerns a recruit who, like the protagonist in *The Things They Carried*, struggles with his fear of cowardice and the "red sickness of battle." Vonnegut's 1969 novel *Slaughterhouse-Five* is about a World War II draftee who is taken as a prisoner-of-war during the Battle of the Bulge. Like Vonnegut, O'Brien inserts himself into his stories—in order to anchor his narratives to a larger world, but also because he is unable to escape the often terrifying memories of his war experience.

Plot Overview

THE PROTAGONIST, who is named Tim O'Brien, begins by describing an event that occurred in the middle of his Vietnam experience. "The Things They Carried" catalogs the variety of things his fellow soldiers in the Alpha Company brought on their missions. Several of these things are intangible, including guilt and fear, while others are specific physical objects, including matches, morphine, M-16 rifles, and M&M's candy.

Throughout the collection, the same characters reappear in various stories. The first member of the Alpha Company to die is Ted Lavender, a "grunt," or low-ranking soldier, who deals with his anxiety about the war by taking tranquilizers and smoking marijuana. Lavender is shot in the head on his way back from going to the bathroom, and his superior, Lieutenant Jimmy Cross, blames himself for the tragedy. When Lavender is shot, Cross is distracting himself with thoughts of Martha, a college crush. It is revealed in "Love" that Cross's feelings for Martha, whom he dated once before leaving for Vietnam, were never reciprocated, and that even twenty years after the war, his guilt over Lavender's death remains.

In "On the Rainy River," the narrator, O'Brien, explains the series of events that led him to Vietnam in the first place. He receives his draft notice in June of 1968, and his feelings of confusion drive him north to the Canadian border, which he contemplates crossing so that he will not be forced to fight in a war in which he doesn't believe. Sitting in a rowboat with the proprietor of the Tip Top Lodge, where he stays, O'Brien decides that his guilt about avoiding the war and fear of disappointing his family are more important than his political convictions. He soon leaves, going first back home to Worthington, Minnesota and later to Vietnam.

In addition to Ted Lavender, a few other members of the Alpha Company are killed during their mission overseas, including Curt Lemon, who is killed when using a grenade to play catch with the medic, Rat Kiley. Though O'Brien is not close to Lemon, in "The Dentist," he tells a story of how Lemon, who faints before a routine checkup with an army-issued dentist, tries to save face by insisting that a perfectly good tooth be pulled. Lee Strunk, another member of the company, dies from injuries he sustains by stepping on a land-mine. In "Friends," O'Brien remembers that before Strunk was fatally hurt, Strunk and Dave Jensen had made a pact that if either man were irreparably harmed, the other man would see that he was quickly killed. However, when Strunk is actually hurt, he begs Jensen to spare him, and Jensen complies. Instead of being upset by the news of his friend's swift death en route to treatment, Jensen is relieved.

The death that receives the most attention in *The Things They Carried* is that of Kiowa, a much-loved member of the Alpha Company and one of O'Brien's closest friends. In "Speaking of Courage," the story of Kiowa's death is relayed in retrospect through the memory of Norman Bowker, years after the war. As Bowker drives around a lake in his Iowa hometown, he thinks that he failed to save Kiowa, who was killed when a mortar round hit and caused him to sink headfirst into a marshy field. O'Brien realizes that he has dealt with his guilt over Kiowa's death differently than Norman Bowker in "Notes." Just before the end of the war, O'Brien receives a long letter from Bowker that says he hasn't found a way to make life meaningful after the war. O'Brien resolves to tell Bowker's story, and the story of Kiowa's death, in order to negotiate his own feelings of guilt and hollowness.

Like "Love" and "Notes," several of O'Brien's stories are told from a perspective twenty years after the Vietnam War, when he is a forty-three-year-old writer living in Massachusetts. Exposure to the guilt of old friends like Jimmy Cross and Norman Bowker prompts him to write stories in order to understand what they were going through. But two stories, "The Man I Killed" and "Ambush," are written so that O'Brien can confront his own guilt over killing a man with a grenade outside the village of My Khe. In "The Man I Killed," O'Brien imagines the life of his victim, from his childhood to the way things would have turned out for him had O'Brien not spotted him on a path and thrown a grenade at his feet. In "Ambush," O'Brien imagines how he might relay the story of the man he killed to his nine-year-old daughter, Kathleen. In this second story, O'Brien provides more details of the actual killing—including the sound of the grenade and his own feelings—and explains that even well after the fact, he hasn't finished sorting out the experience.

In the last story, "The Lives of the Dead," O'Brien gives another twist to his contention that stories have the power to save people. In the stories of Curt Lemon and Kiowa, O'Brien explains that his imagination allowed him to grapple successfully with his guilt and confusion over the death of his fourth-grade first love, Linda.

Character List

Tim O'Brien The narrator and protagonist of the collection of stories. O'Brien is a pacifist who rationalizes his participation in Vietnam by concluding that his feelings of obligation toward his family and country are stronger influences than his own politics. When the war is over, he uses his ability to tell stories to deal with his guilt and confusion over the atrocities he witnessed in Vietnam, including the death of several of his fellow soldiers and of a Viet Cong soldier by his own hand.

Jimmy Cross The lieutenant of the Alpha Company, who is responsible for the entire group of men. Cross is well intentioned but unsure of how to lead his men. He is wracked with guilt because he believes that his preoccupation with his unrequited love for a girl named Martha and his tendency to follow orders despite his better judgment caused the deaths of Ted Lavender and Kiowa, two members of Alpha Company.

Mitchell Sanders One of the most likable soldiers in the war. Sanders strongly influences the narrator, O'Brien. He is kind and devoted, and he has a strong sense of justice. Because of these qualities, he is a type of father figure. Though his ideas of storytelling may or may not agree with O'Brien's in the end, his ability to tell stories and to discuss their nuances makes a profound impression on O'Brien.

Kiowa O'Brien's closest friend and a model of quiet, rational morality amid the atrocities of war. Kiowa's death, when the company mistakenly camps in a sewage field, is the focal point of three stories. Since it is a prime example of arbitrary, unforgiving cruelty in war, Kiowa's death is given more prominence than his life.

Norman Bowker A man who embodies the damage that the war can do to a soldier long after the war is over. During the war, Bowker is quiet and unassuming, and Kiowa's death has a profound effect on him. Bowker's letter to O'Brien in "Notes" demonstrates the importance of sharing stories in the healing process.

Henry Dobbins The platoon's machine gunner and resident gentle giant. Dobbins's profound decency, despite his simplicity, contrasts with his bearish frame. He is a perfect example of the incongruities in Vietnam.

Bob "Rat" Kiley The platoon's medic. Kiley previously served in the mountains of Chu Lai, the setting of "Sweetheart of the Song Tra Bong." O'Brien has great respect for Kiley's medical prowess, especially when he is shot for a second time and is subjected to the mistreatment of another medic, Bobby Jorgenson. Though levelheaded and kind, Kiley eventually succumbs to the stresses of the war and his role in it—he purposely blows off his toe so that he is forced to leave his post.

Curt Lemon A childish and careless member of the Alpha Company who is killed while tossing a grenade in a game of catch. Though O'Brien does not particularly like Lemon, Lemon's death is something O'Brien continually contemplates with sadness and regret. The preventability of his death and the irrational fears of his life—as when a dentist visits the company—point to the immaturity of many young American soldiers in Vietnam.

Ted Lavender A young, scared soldier in the Alpha Company. Lavender is the first to die in the work. He makes only a brief appearance in the narrative, popping tranquilizers to calm himself while the company is outside Than Khe. Because his death, like Lemon's, is preventable, it illustrates the expendability of human life in a senseless war.

Lee Strunk Another soldier in the platoon and a minor character. A struggle with Dave Jensen over a jackknife results in Strunk's broken nose. In begging Jensen to forget their pact—that if either man is gravely injured, the other will kill him swiftly—after he is injured, he illustrates how the fantasy of war differs from its reality.

Dave Jensen A minor character whose guilt over his injury of Lee Strunk causes him to break his own nose. Jensen's relief after Strunk's death is an illustration of the perspective soldiers are forced to assume. Instead of mourning the loss of his friend, Jensen is glad to know that the pact the two made—and that he broke—has now become obsolete.

Azar A soldier in the Alpha Company and one of the few unsympathetic characters in the work. Every time Azar appears, he is mean-spirited and cruel, torturing Vietnamese civilians and poking fun both at the corpses of the enemy and the deaths of his own fellow soldiers. His humanity is finally demonstrated near the end of the work, when he is forced to help unearth Kiowa's body from the muck of the sewage field. This moment of remorse proves that a breaking point is possible even for soldiers who use cruelty as a defense mechanism.

Bobby Jorgenson The medic who replaces Rat Kiley. The second time O'Brien is shot, Jorgenson's incompetence inspires O'Brien's desire for irrational revenge. Although Jorgenson's anger prompts him to kick O'Brien in the head for trying to scare him, he later apologizes, redeeming himself as a medic by patching things up with O'Brien.

Elroy Berdahl The proprietor of the Tip Top Lodge on the Rainy River near the Canadian border. Berdahl serves as the closest thing to a father figure for O'Brien, who, after receiving his draft notice, spends six contemplative days with the quiet, kind Berdahl while he makes a decision about whether to go to war or to escape the draft by running across the border to Canada.

Kathleen   O'Brien's daughter and a symbol of the naïve outsider. Although O'Brien alludes to having multiple children, Kathleen is the only one we meet. Her youth and innocence force O'Brien to try to explain the meaning of the war. Frustrated that he cannot tell her the whole truth, he is inspired by her presence since it forces him to gain new perspective on his war experience.

Mary Anne Bell   Mark Fossie's high school sweetheart. Although Mary Anne arrives in Vietnam full of innocence, she gains a respect for death and the darkness of the jungle and, according to legend, disappears there. Unlike Martha and Henry Dobbins's girlfriend, who only serve as fantasy reminders of a world removed from Vietnam, Mary Anne is a strong and realized character who shatters Fossie's fantasy of finding comfort in his docile girlfriend.

Mark Fossie   A medic in Rat Kiley's previous assignment. Fossie loses his innocence in the realization that his girlfriend, Mary Anne, would rather be out on ambush with Green Berets than planning her postwar wedding to Fossie in Cleveland.

Linda   O'Brien's first love, whose death of a brain tumor in the fifth grade is O'Brien's first experience with mortality. From his experience with Linda, O'Brien learns the power that storytelling has to keep memory alive.

Analysis of Major Characters

Tim O'Brien

Tim O'Brien is both the narrator and protagonist of *The Things They Carried*. The work recounts his personal experience in the Vietnam War and allows him to comment on the war. He enters the war a scared young man afraid of the shame that dodging the war would bring him and leaves the war a guilt-ridden middle-aged man who tells stories about Vietnam in order to cope with his painful memories. To cover the distance between himself and what he recounts, O'Brien weaves a prominent thread of memory through the work. Reading these stories is similar to spending extended time with an old soldier, allowing his memories to come to him slowly.

O'Brien's point of view shapes the events he relates. In many, if not most, cases, O'Brien holds himself up as evidence for the generalizations he makes about the war. He is our guide through the inexplicable horror of the war and the main example of how extreme situations can turn a rationally thinking man into a soldier who commits unspeakable acts and desires cruel and irrational things. Occasionally, O'Brien fades away and lets another character or a seemingly omniscient third person tell the story. This technique lends a universal human quality to the stories' themes and gives us the opportunity to understand the Alpha Company from several different perspectives.

O'Brien uses storytelling as solace and as a means of coming to terms with the unspeakable horrors he witnessed as a soldier. His comments suggest that although he has become a successful writer and that his negotiation of memory through storytelling has been a good coping mechanism, he still thinks that certain realities cannot be explained at all. His experience with those untouched by the war, such as his daughter Kathleen, exposes an irony in his faith in storytelling. He knows that he can grapple with his feelings of disbelief and painful confusion by telling others what happened and how, but he cannot express every feeling.

Jimmy Cross

Jimmy Cross's character represents the profound effects responsibility has on those who are too immature to handle it. As a sophomore in college, he signs up for the Reserve Officers Training Corps because it is worth a few credits and because his friends are doing it. But he doesn't care about the war and has no desire to be a team leader. As a result, when he is led into battle with several men in his charge, he is unsure in everything he does.

Cross's guilt is palpable every time one of his men dies, but it is most acute in the case of Ted Lavender. Right before Lavender is killed, Cross allows himself to be distracted and deluded by the thoughts of his coveted classmate, Martha, who sends him photographs and writes flowery letters that never mention the war. His innocent reverie is interrupted by Lavender's death, and Cross's only conclusion is that he loves this faraway girl more than he loves his men. Cross's confession to O'Brien, years later, that he has never forgiven himself for Lavender's death testifies to his intense feelings of guilt about the incident.

Jimmy Cross can be viewed as a Christ figure. In times of inexplicable atrocity, certain individuals assume the position of a group's or their own savior. Such men suffer so that others don't have to bear the brunt of the guilt and confusion. Cross is linked to Christ not only on a superficial level—they share initials and are both connected to the idea of the cross—but also in the nature of his role. Like Christ, who suffers for his fellow men, Cross suffers for the sake of the entire platoon. In "The Things They Carried," Cross bears the grief of Lavender's death for the members of his troop, such as Kiowa, who are too dumbfounded to mourn. In the same story, he makes a personal sacrifice, burning the letters from Martha so that her presence will no longer distract him. In each case, Cross makes a Christ-like sacrifice so that his fellow men—Norman Bowker and Kiowa, in this case—can carry on without being crippled by grief and guilt.

Mitchell Sanders

Mitchell Sanders is a likable soldier and a devoted friend. He has a sense of irony, picking lice off his body and sending them back to his draft board in Ohio, and a sense of loyalty, refusing to help O'Brien inflict revenge on the medic Bobby Jorgenson and standing by Rat

Kiley in his decision to escape Vietnam by shooting himself in the toe. He also has a strong sense of justice—when Cross leads the troops into the sewage field where Kiowa eventually meets his death, Sanders refuses to forgive him because the evidence shows that he should have known better.

Sanders often applies this pragmatism to his storytelling. He believes that a good war story often lacks a moral and that sometimes a story without commentary or explanation speaks for itself because he understands that war stories are never simple or cut-and-dried. In his story about the platoon driven crazy by phantom voices in the jungle, for example, he offers no explanation of what the voices were. Instead, he focuses on the soldiers' experience of the voices, which he considers more relevant and concrete. Sanders is in this way a mouthpiece for O'Brien, who presents the stories that constitute *The Things They Carried* not to teach a moral but to portray an experience.

KIOWA

In life, Kiowa is diligent and honest, introspective and compassionate. He is practical, carrying moccasins in order to be able to walk silently and helping his fellow soldiers to rationalize their own unfortunate actions, especially O'Brien's killing of a young Vietnamese soldier. A Baptist and a Native American, he brings a perspective different from that of his fellow soldiers to the unfortunate events that befall the Alpha Company.

Kiowa's death is symbolic of the senseless tragedy of war. He dies in a gruesome way, drowning under the muck of a sewage field about which his lieutenant, Jimmy Cross, has a bad feeling. Kiowa's entirely submerged body represents the transitory nature of life and the horrifying suddenness with which it can be snatched away. There is no dignity to Kiowa's death; he becomes another casualty in a war that strips men of their identity and turns them into statistics.

Themes, Motifs & Symbols

Themes

Themes are the fundamental and often universal ideas explored in a literary work.

Physical and Emotional Burdens

The "[t]hings" of the title that O'Brien's characters carry are both literal and figurative. While they all carry heavy physical loads, they also all carry heavy emotional loads, composed of grief, terror, love, and longing. Each man's physical burden underscores his emotional burden. Henry Dobbins, for example, carries his girlfriend's pantyhose and, with them, the longing for love and comfort. Similarly, Jimmy Cross carries compasses and maps and, with them, the responsibility for the men in his charge. Faced with the heavy burden of fear, the men also carry the weight of their reputations. Although every member of the Alpha Company experiences fear at some point, showing fear will only reveal vulnerability to both the enemy and sometimes cruel fellow soldiers.

After the war, the psychological burdens the men carry during the war continue to define them. Those who survive carry guilt, grief, and confusion, and many of the stories in the collection are about these survivors' attempts to come to terms with their experience. In "Love," for example, Jimmy Cross confides in O'Brien that he has never forgiven himself for Ted Lavender's death. Norman Bowker's grief and confusion are so strong that they prompt him to drive aimlessly around his hometown lake in "Speaking of Courage," to write O'Brien a seventeen-page letter explaining how he never felt right after the war in "Notes," and to hang himself in a YMCA. While Bowker bears his psychological burdens alone, O'Brien shares the things he carries, his war stories, with us. His collection of stories asks us to help carry the burden of the Vietnam War as part of our collective past.

Fear of Shame as Motivation

O'Brien's personal experience shows that the fear of being shamed before one's peers is a powerful motivating factor in war. His story "On the Rainy River" explains his moral quandary after receiving his draft notice—he does not want to fight in a war he believes is unjust, but he does not want to be thought a coward. What keeps O'Brien from fleeing into Canada is not patriotism or dedication to his country's cause—the traditional motivating factors for fighting in a war—but concern over what his family and community will think of him if he doesn't fight. This experience is emblematic of the conflict, explored throughout *The Things They Carried*, between the misguided expectations of a group of people important to a character and that character's uncertainty regarding a proper course of action.

Fear of shame not only motivates reluctant men to go to Vietnam but also affects soldiers' relationships with each other once there. Concern about social acceptance, which might seem in the abstract an unimportant preoccupation given the immediacy of death and necessity of group unity during war, leads O'Brien's characters to engage in absurd or dangerous actions. For example, Curt Lemon decides to have a perfectly good tooth pulled (in "The Dentist") to ease his shame about having fainted during an earlier encounter with the dentist. The stress of the war, the strangeness of Vietnam, and the youth of the soldiers combine to create psychological dangers that intensify the inherent risks of fighting. Jimmy Cross, who has gone to war only because his friends have, becomes a confused and uncertain leader who endangers the lives of his soldiers. O'Brien uses these characters to show that fear of shame is a misguided but unavoidable motivation for going to war.

The Subjection of Truth to Storytelling

By giving the narrator his own name and naming the rest of his characters after the men he actually fought alongside in the Vietnam War, O'Brien blurs the distinction between fact and fiction. The result is that it is impossible to know whether or not any given event in the stories truly happened to O'Brien. He intentionally heightens this impossibility when his characters contradict themselves several times in the collection of stories, rendering the truth of any statement suspect. O'Brien's aim in blending fact and fiction is to make the point that objective truth of a war story is less relevant than the act of telling a story. O'Brien is attempting not to write a history of the Vietnam War through his stories but rather to explore the ways that speaking about war experience establishes or fails to establish bonds between a soldier and his audience. The technical facts surrounding any individual event are less important than the overarching, subjective truth of what the war meant to soldiers and how it changed them.

The different storytellers in *The Things They Carried*—Rat Kiley and Mitchell Sanders especially, in addition to O'Brien—work to lay out war's ugly truths, which are so profound that they require neither facts nor long explanations. Such statements as "This is true," which opens "How to Tell a True War Story," do not establish that the events recounted in the story actually occurred. Rather, they indicate that the stylistic and thematic content of the story is true to the experience that the soldiers had in the war. This truth is often ugly, in contrast to the ideas of glory and heroism associated with war before Vietnam. In O'Brien's "true" war story, Kiley writes to Lemon's sister, and when she never responds, he calls her a "dumb cooze," only adding to the ugliness of the story. O'Brien's declaration that the truest part of this story is that it contains no moral underscores the idea that the purpose of stories is to relate the truth of experience, not to manufacture false emotions in their audiences.

Motifs

Motifs are recurring structures, contrasts, or literary devices that can help to develop and inform the text's major themes.

Storytelling

O'Brien believes that stories contain immense power, since they allow tellers and listeners to confront the past together and share otherwise unknowable experiences. Telling stories returns to the foreground of the narrative again and again. Mitchell Sanders, the Alpha Company's resident storyteller, whose anecdotes range from the mythic (the story of six men who hear voices in the jungle) to the specific (the story of how Rat Kiley shoots himself in the foot and as a result is allowed to leave Vietnam), contends that truth and morality in a war story have little to do with accuracy. For example, after telling the story of the men who hear voices in the jungle, Sanders admits that he made up a few things in order to get his point across. Nevertheless, his story has resonance. The added details are only further proof of the universal truth: the eerie quiet of the jungle causes soldiers' imaginations to run wild with fantastic images far stranger than anything they might actually encounter.

O'Brien shows that storytelling is not just a coping mechanism for soldiers who are embroiled in the war but also a strategy for communication throughout life. Several of the stories in *The Things They Carried* are told from O'Brien's point of view, twenty years after the war. With this distance, facts have become cloudy and all that remains of the experience are the lingering feelings and memories. He is aware of his omissions and exaggeration of detail, and in the case of "Good Form," he even suggests that all of his previous stories are made up. Even if he did not actually kill a soldier in My Khe, the truth of his feelings about war is no less valid. His insistence on the idea that stories can make the past become part of the present shows that his priority is not on the facts but on our identification with his feelings.

Ambiguous Morality

O'Brien's stories show that the jungle blurs boundaries between right and wrong. The brutal killing of innocents on both sides cannot be explained, and in some moments of disbelief, the men deal with the pain of their feelings by pointing out the irony. "There's a moral here," Mitchell Sanders ironically points out again and again, each time stressing the actual immorality of the specific situation. After Ted Lavender is fatally shot by the enemy, for example, Sanders jokes that the "moral" of Ted Lavender's accidental and tragic death is to stay away from drugs.

Exposed to these horrors, the men's notions of right and wrong shift and bend. After Ted Lavender's death, for example, Cross evens the score and deals with his own guilt by burning the entire village of Than Khe. Similarly, Rat Kiley deals with his frustration about Curt Lemon's death by brutally killing a water buffalo. Affected by the senselessness of war, even O'Brien—a college educated, peace-loving man—feels himself grow hard and callous, willing to wish others harm. Ironically, the moral or lesson in *The Things They Carried* is that there is no morality in war. War is ambiguous and arbitrary because it forces humans into extreme situations that have no obvious solutions.

Loneliness and Isolation

O'Brien argues that in Vietnam, loneliness and isolation are forces as destructive as any piece of ammunition. In repeatedly emphasizing the impact of solitude on the soldiers, he shows that thoughts, worries, and fears are as dangerous—if not more dangerous—than the Vietnamese soldiers themselves. In "How to Tell a True War Story," Mitchell Sanders's story concerning soldiers made so paranoid by their experience on listening patrol that they hear strange noises emphasizes how the imagination can take over instantly in the lonely silence. In "The Ghost Soldiers," O'Brien takes unfair advantage of the power of isolation when he attempts to frighten Bobby Jorgenson while Jorgenson is on night guard duty. In order to emphasize the evil intentions of his revenge plot, O'Brien reflects on his fear of being cut off from the outside world and the close relation between night guard and childhood fears of the dark. In Vietnam, isolation is synonymous with endless time to dwell on the unknown.

Loneliness remains a strong presence enveloping the soldiers long after the war is over. Jimmy Cross, for example, feels bereft after the war because his hope for happiness in Martha is dashed by her rejection. Norman Bowker also feels empty and isolated after the war. In "Speaking of Courage," he aimlessly drives around a lake in his hometown, thinking that he has no one to talk to. He even attempts to converse with an A&W employee, but no one will offer him consolation. O'Brien himself realizes that if he didn't have writing to work through his trauma, he might be in as abject a place as Bowker. The character O'Brien's narration—and, in effect, the author O'Brien's *The Things They Carried*—is an attempt to combat the destructive isolation that the Vietnam experience fostered.

Symbols

Symbols are objects, characters, figures, or colors used to represent abstract ideas or concepts.

The Dead Young Vietnamese Soldier

Although O'Brien is unclear about whether or not he actually threw a grenade and killed a man outside My Khe, his memory of the man's corpse is strong and recurring, symbolizing humanity's guilt over war's horrible acts. In "The Man I Killed," O'Brien distances himself from the memory by speaking in the third person and constructing fantasies as to what the man must have been like before he was killed. O'Brien marvels at the wreckage of his body, thinking repeatedly of the star-shaped hole that is in the place of his eye and the peeled-back cheek. The description serves to distance O'Brien from the reality of his actions because nowhere in its comprehensive detail are O'Brien's feelings about the situation mentioned. His guilt is evident, however, in his imagining of a life for the man he killed that includes several aspects that are similar to his own life.

Kathleen

Kathleen represents a reader who has the capability of responding to the author. Like us, O'Brien's daughter Kathleen is often the recipient of O'Brien's war stories, but unlike us, she can affect O'Brien as much as O'Brien affects her. O'Brien gains a new perspective on his experiences in Vietnam when he thinks about how he should relay the story of the man he killed to his impressionable young daughter.

Kathleen also stands for the gap in communication between one who tells a story and one who receives a story. When O'Brien takes her to Vietnam to have her better understand what he went through during the war, the only things that resonate to the ten-year-old are the stink of the muck and the strangeness of the land. She has no sense of the field's emotional significance to O'Brien, and thus does not understand his behavior there, as when he goes for a swim.

Linda

Linda represents elements of the past that can be brought back through imagination and storytelling. Linda, a classmate of O'Brien's who died of a brain tumor in the fifth grade, symbolizes O'Brien's faith that storytelling is the best way for him to negotiate pain and confusion, especially the sadness that surrounds death. Linda was O'Brien's first love and also his first experience with death's senseless arbitrariness. His retreat into his daydreams after her funeral provided him unexpected relief and rationalization. In his dreams, he could see Linda still alive, which suggests that through imagination—which, for O'Brien, later evolves into storytelling—the dead can continue to live.

Linda's presence in the story makes O'Brien's earlier stories about Vietnam more universal. The experience he had as a child illuminates the way he deals with death in Vietnam and after; it also explains why he has turned to stories to deal with life's difficulties. Just like Linda, Norman Bowker and Kiowa are immortalized in O'Brien's stories. Their commonplace lives become more significant than their dramatic deaths. Through the image of Linda, O'Brien realizes that he continues to save his own life through storytelling.

Summary & Analysis

"The Things They Carried"

> *Men killed, and died, because they were embarrassed not to.* (See QUOTATIONS, p. 67)

Summary

Lieutenant Jimmy Cross, of the Alpha Company, carries various reminders of his love for Martha, a girl from his college in New Jersey who has given no indication of returning his love. Cross carries her letters in his backpack and her good-luck pebble in his mouth. After a long day's march, he unwraps her letters and imagines the prospect of her returning his love someday. Martha is an English major who writes letters that quote lines of poetry and never mention the war. Though the letters are signed "Love, Martha" Cross understands that this gesture should not give him false hope. He wonders, uncontrollably, about whether or not Martha is a virgin. He carries her photographs, including one of her playing volleyball, but closer to his heart still are his memories. They went on a single date, to see the movie *Bonnie and Clyde*. When Cross touched Martha's knee during the final scene, Martha looked at him and made him pull his hand back. Now, in Vietnam, Cross wishes that he had carried her up the stairs, tied her to the bed, and touched her knee all night long. He is haunted by the cutting knowledge that his affection will most likely never be returned.

The narrator, Tim O'Brien, describes the things all the men of the company carry. They are things in the most physical sense—mosquito repellent and marijuana, pocket knives and chewing gum. The things they carry depend on several factors, including the men's priorities and their constitutions. Because the machine gunner Henry Dobbins is exceptionally large, for example, he carries extra rations; because he is superstitious, he carries his girlfriend's pantyhose around his neck. Nervous Ted Lavender carries marijuana and tranquilizers to calm himself down, and the religious Kiowa carries an illustrated New Testament, a gift from his father.

Some things the men carry are universal, like a compress in case of fatal injuries and a two-pound poncho that can be used as a raincoat, groundsheet, or tent. Most of the men are common, low-ranking soldiers and carry a standard M-16 assault rifle and several magazines of ammunition. Several men carry grenade launchers. All men carry the figurative weight of memory and the literal weight of one another. They carry Vietnam itself, in the heavy weather and the dusty soil. The things they carry are also determined by their rank or specialty. As leader, for example, Lieutenant Jimmy Cross carries the maps, the compasses, and the responsibility for his men's lives. The medic, Rat Kiley, carries morphine, malaria tablets, and supplies for serious wounds.

One day, when the company outside the Than Khe area is on a mission to destroy tunnel complexes, Cross imagines the tunnels collapsing on him and Martha. He becomes distracted by wondering whether or not she is a virgin. On the way back from going to the bathroom, Lavender is shot, falling especially hard under the burden of his loaded backpack. Still, Cross can think of nothing but Martha. He thinks about her love of poetry and her smooth skin.

While the soldiers wait for the helicopter to carry Lavender's body away, they smoke his marijuana. They make jokes about Lavender's tranquilizer abuse and rationalize that he probably was too numb to feel pain when he was shot. Cross leads his men to the village of Than Khe—where the soldiers burn everything and shoot dogs and chickens—and then on a march through the late afternoon heat. When they stop for the evening, Cross digs a foxhole in the ground and sits at the bottom of it, crying. Meanwhile, Kiowa and Norman Bowker sit in the darkness discussing the short span between life and death in an attempt to make sense of the situation. In the ensuing silence, Kiowa marvels at how Lavender fell so quickly and how he was zipping up his pants one second and dead the next. He finds something unchristian about the lack of drama surrounding this type of death and wonders why he cannot openly lament it like Cross does.

The morning after Lavender's death, in the steady rain, Cross crouches in his foxhole and burns Martha's letters and two photographs. He plans the day's march and concludes that he will never again have fantasies. He plans to call the men together and assume the blame for Lavender's death. He reminds himself that, despite the men's inevitable grumbling, his job is not to be loved but to lead.

Analysis

O'Brien uses the list of physical objects that the members of the Alpha Company carry in Vietnam as a window to the emotional burdens that these soldiers bear. One such burden is the necessity for the young soldiers to confront the tension between fantasy and reality. The realization of this tension disrupts Cross's stint as the resident dreamer of the Alpha Company. Cross thinks that because he was so obsessed with his fantasy of Martha and the life they might lead after the war, he was negligent. He sees Ted Lavender's death as the result of his negligence. If "The Things They Carried" is the illustration of the conflict between love and war, then the death of Ted Lavender and the subsequent disillusionment of Lieutenant Cross signify a triumph for war in this conflict.

Cross's reaction to Ted Lavender's death shows how the horrors of the war can make men irreparably cynical and gloomy. Before Lavender's death, the most vivid images Cross carries in his mind are those of Martha. He is obsessed with trivial matters such as whether or not she is a virgin and why she so tantalizingly signs her letters "Love." But when he decides his thoughts of her have led him astray and that they—and she—caused the distraction and incompetence that led to Lavender's death, he expresses his anger at her in the only way possible. He burns Martha's pictures and letters in an attempt to distance himself from the sentimentality he sees as a destructive force during wartime. His conclusion, at the end of this story, that it is better to be loved than to lead, reveals how the experience of Lavender's death has affected his mentality.

The emotional burdens that the soldiers bear are intensified by their young age and inexperience. Most of the men who fought in Vietnam were in their late teens and early twenties—they were children, students, and boyfriends who had no perspective on how to rationalize killing or come to terms with their friends' untimely deaths. From the beginning, O'Brien the author uses explicit details to illustrate what the experience was like for the scared men. Among the things the men carry are guilt and cowardice that they are neither able to admit to nor negotiate. Although they are sad for the loss of their friend Lavender, their predominant feeling is of relief, since they are still alive.

O'Brien's decision to intersperse profound thoughts with mundane events establishes the matter-of-fact tone of the collection. The collection's narrative alternates between reflections on war and the story of Ted Lavender's death. By arranging the work this way,

O'Brien uses facts to create setting. He explicitly demonstrates his characters' natures not by describing them but by showing the items they carried with them in such dire circumstances. Rather than explain Kiowa's heritage in concrete terms, for example, O'Brien simply mentions that Kiowa carries his grandfather's hatchet and an illustrated New Testament. O'Brien here offers us glimpses of characters whose traits become integral to the ideas that O'Brien explores throughout *The Things They Carried*.

"LOVE"

SUMMARY

Years after the end of the war, Jimmy Cross goes to visit Tim O'Brien at his home in Massachusetts. They drink coffee and smoke cigarettes, looking at photographs and reminiscing. When they come across a picture of Ted Lavender, Cross confesses that he has never forgiven himself for Lavender's death. O'Brien comforts him by saying that he feels the same way about other things, and the two men switch from coffee to gin. They steer the conversation away from the more harsh memories and laugh about less upsetting recollections, such as the way Henry Dobbins used to carry his girlfriend's pantyhose around his neck as a good-luck charm. Finally, by the end of the night, O'Brien thinks it's safe to ask about Martha.

Cross tells O'Brien that when he finally reconnected with Martha at a college reunion in 1979, they spent most of their time together, catching up. She had become a Lutheran missionary and had done service in Ethiopia, Guatemala, and Mexico. She had never married and told Cross she didn't know why. Later, Cross took her hand, but Martha didn't squeeze back; when he told her he loved her, she didn't answer. Finally Cross told her that the night of their only date, after they watched *Bonnie and Clyde*, all he'd wanted to do was to take her home and tie her to her bed so he could touch her knee all night long. Martha replied coldly that she didn't understand how men could do such things. At breakfast the next morning, she apologized and gave him another snapshot, telling him not to burn this one.

Cross tells O'Brien that he still loves Martha. But for the rest of his visit with O'Brien, he doesn't speak of her. Finally, as O'Brien walks Cross to his car, he tells his former lieutenant that he would like to write a story about some of what they have spoken about. After some consideration, Cross consents, saying that maybe Martha will read it and come begging for him. He urges O'Brien to paint him as a brave and good leader. He then asks O'Brien for a favor—that he not "mention anything about—." O'Brien responds that he won't.

ANALYSIS

"Love" functions as a postscript or epilogue for the story of Jimmy Cross and Martha, begun in the previous story, "The Things They Carried." O'Brien's explanation of how things turned out for Cross and Martha, twenty years after the war, is his first reference to the fallout of Vietnam. When the war ended, soldiers returned home to realize the dreams they had put on hold during the war. However, what was waiting for them in the end wasn't always what they hoped it would be. Cross put his faith in Martha because he couldn't put his faith in war itself and because the notion of her as a sexual being and as someone who might want to start a life with him upon his return was safe and comforting.

The meaning of the title "Love" is complicated because Cross is both skeptical of the word and hopeful that it carries meaning in Martha's letters. Cross's skepticism becomes clear early on; when he reads Martha's letters in an effort to distract himself from the atrocities and unknowns he faces in the jungle, he suspects that the "Love" with which she signs her letters is merely a figure of speech. When the details are filled in years after the fact, the truth of the word "Love" is revealed—Martha never loved Cross. In effect, this realization makes only more profound the impact of Lavender's death on the already guilt-ridden Cross. Whether Martha is uninterested because she is incapable of love, because Cross's obsession with her eventually turned her off, or because the time in which she came of age was filled with such abject disillusionment, Cross is injured—he needs gin to prompt him into speaking, and he doesn't want to linger too long on the topic.

Through Cross's character, O'Brien shows how repression of painful memories can be essential for survival. Cross carries a haunting secret with him from his experience leading the Alpha Company, but O'Brien leaves the nature of the secret ambiguous. Informed by the previous story, we assume that the secret is Cross's lingering guilt over Lavender's death, but O'Brien not only refuses to name it, he actually obscures Cross's naming of the secret at the end of "Love."

O'Brien's narrative strategies reflect the repression that his characters practice. O'Brien himself is unwilling to communicate fully with his readers, which makes it unclear whether or not he is reliable. It is unclear, for instance, whether O'Brien's conversation with Cross actually happened or whether it is a fiction that renders "The Things They Carried" more realistic. Though the distinction is not made in this story, or in any of the others, the resemblance between O'Brien the author and O'Brien the main character is one of several attempts O'Brien makes to raise the stakes of his storytelling and to inspire our investment in his stories. The distinction between truth and fiction does not mean much to O'Brien; feelings behind the story give the narrative its purpose. Therefore, whether or not O'Brien betrayed Cross is irrelevant when compared to the impact of Cross's feelings of guilt.

The ambiguous ending of "Love" is symptomatic of the difficulty war veterans have in vocalizing traumatic experiences. We cannot be sure if the thing Cross asks O'Brien not to mention has been put in the story or not. Perhaps O'Brien has betrayed his friend and the thing Cross requested he not mention is his guilt over Ted Lavender's death or his relationship with and eventual rejection by Martha. Or perhaps O'Brien is faithful to Cross's wishes and the thing he is asked not to mention is kept from us the entire time. No matter what Cross's secret is, O'Brien's ambiguities force us to consider the act of writing as a way of conveying the conflicting motivations involved in making difficult decisions.

"Spin"

Summary

Insisting that sometimes war is less violent and more sweet, O'Brien shares disconnected memories of the war. Azar gives a bar of chocolate to a little boy with a plastic leg. Mitchell Sanders sits under a tree, picking lice off his body and depositing them in an envelope addressed to his Ohio draft board. Every night, Henry Dobbins and Norman Bowker dig a foxhole and play checkers. The narrator stops the string of anecdotes to say that he is now forty-three years old and a writer, and that reliving the memories has caused them to recur. He insists that the bad memories live on and never stop happening. He says his guilt has not ceased and that his daughter Kathleen advises him to write about something else. Nevertheless, he says, writing about what one remembers is a means of coping with those things one can't forget.

O'Brien describes when the Alpha Company enlists an old Vietnamese man whom they call a "poppa-san" to guide the platoon through the mine fields on the Batangan Peninsula. When he is done, the troops are sad to leave their steadfast guide. Mitchell Sanders tells a story of a man who went AWOL in order to sleep with a Red Cross nurse. After several days, the man rejoined his unit and was more excited than ever about getting back into combat, saying that after so much peace, he wanted to hurt again. Norman Bowker whispers one night that if he could have one wish it would be for his father to stop bothering him about earning medals. Kiowa teaches Rat Kiley and Dave Jensen a rain dance, and when they ask him, afterward, where the rain was, he replies, "The earth is slow, but the buffalo is patient." Ted Lavender adopts a puppy, and Azar later kills it, claiming his own immaturity as an excuse. Henry Dobbins sings to himself as he sews on his new buck-sergeant stripes. Lavender occasionally goes too heavy on the tranquilizers and calls the war "nice" and "mellow." After Curt Lemon is killed, he hangs in pieces on a tree. Last comes the vision of a dead, young man and Kiowa's voice ringing in O'Brien's ear, assuring him, repeatedly, that O'Brien didn't have a choice.

Analysis

"Spin," with its unconnected anecdotes delivered in scattered phrases and half-realized memories, stylistically echoes the fragmentation of the war experience. Like the anecdotes in "The Things They Carried," the anecdotes here are static and seemingly unrelated. They jump in time, purpose, and magnitude in the same way that a soldier's mind might jump around his past. In this story, it becomes clear to us that all the stories O'Brien is telling originate from his memory. A shift in tone accompanies the fragmentation; O'Brien transitions from a balanced to a disillusioned evaluation of the war. He argues that the war is unlike Dobbins and Bowker's well-ordered, rational games of checkers. The war has neither rules nor winners, and men witness horrific acts juxtaposed with random acts of kindness.

"Spin" is like a map of the uncharted territory of war for readers who have never experienced it. The story allows us to feel the boredom of war by describing the things that happen when nothing is happening: jibes, songs, stomachaches, and despair. It also addresses the way men choose to deal with fright, uncertainty, and devastation. Unable to cope with stress, Azar brutally kills Ted Lavender's adopted puppy and uses his immaturity and youth as an excuse for his actions. O'Brien's decision not to explain or elaborate on this event conveys the message that sometimes the facts in a true war story need no further commentary.

Although the plot of "Spin" is not complicated, the story establishes the identities of the characters who appear throughout *The Things They Carried*. We encounter most of the main characters in the title story, but we find out more about them here. We see the immature inhumanity of Azar, the philosophical even-headedness of Kiowa, and the dimness of Norman Bowker, and each character becomes more rounded and real with the revelation of a new detail. One way that "Spin" develops characters is by describing the inner conflicts that define them throughout *The Things They Carried*. O'Brien revisits, throughout the work, such elements as Ted Lavender's tranquilizer abuse, Curt Lemon's death, and his own killing of a Vietnamese man, and with each new look at a given event we gain added perspective on the characters involved.

O'Brien's relationship with his daughter Kathleen reveals the importance of storytelling. An outsider to O'Brien's experience, Kathleen cannot begin to imagine what her father went through when he was a soldier in a foreign country long before she was born. She is therefore convinced that her father's obsession with Vietnam is an easily curable condition. She suggests that he write something happier, something entirely different, failing to realize that there is a reason that he needs to tell these stories, and to tell them to her, specifically. O'Brien says the function of telling stories is delivering the past into the future, for giving perspective and understanding. His act of telling, which bridges the gap between past and present, helps both him and Kathleen more fully understand his war experience.

"On the Rainy River"

Summary

O'Brien says he has not told this story to his parents, siblings, or wife. He speaks of living with the shame of the story, whose events occurred during the summer of 1968. On June 17, 1968, a month after he graduates from Macalaster College, Phi Beta Kappa, summa cum laude, and president of the student body, Tim O'Brien receives his draft notice to fight in the Vietnam War. The war seems wrong to him, its causes and effects uncertain. Like most Americans, the young O'Brien doesn't know what happened to the USS *Maddox* in the Gulf of Tonkin, and he can't discern what type of person Ho Chi Minh, the president of North Vietnam, really is. In college, O'Brien took a stand against the war.

The day the draft notice is delivered, O'Brien thinks that he is too good to fight the war. Although his community pressures him to go, he resists making a decision about whether to go to war or flee. He spends the summer in a meatpacking plant in his hometown of Worthington, Minnesota, removing blood clots from pigs with a water gun. He comes home every night stinking of pig and drives around town aimlessly, paralyzed, wondering how to find a way out of his situation. It seems to him that there is no easy way out. The government won't allow him to defer in order to go to graduate school; he can't oppose the war as a matter of general principle because he does agree with war in some circumstances; and he can't claim ill health as an excuse. He resents his hometown for making him feel compelled to fight a war that it doesn't even know anything about.

In the middle of the summer, O'Brien begins thinking seriously about fleeing to Canada, eight hours north of Worthington. His conscience and instincts tell him to run. He worries, however, that such an action will lose him the respect of his family and community. He imagines the people he knows gossiping about him in the local café. During his sleepless nights, he struggles with his anger at the lack of perspective on the part of those who influenced him.

One day, O'Brien cracks. Feeling what he describes as a physical rupture in his chest, he leaves work suddenly, drives home, and writes a vague note to his family. He heads north and then west along the Rainy River, which separates Minnesota from Canada. The next afternoon, after spending the night behind a closed-down gas station, he pulls into a dilapidated fishing resort, the Tip Top Lodge, and meets the elderly proprietor, Elroy Berdahl. The two spend six days together, eating meals, hiking, and playing Scrabble. Although O'Brien never mentions his reason for going to the Canadian border, he has the sense that Elroy knows, since the quiet old man is sharp and intelligent. One night O'Brien inquires about his bill, and after the two men discuss O'Brien's work—washing dishes and doing odd jobs—in relation to the cost of the room, Elroy concludes that he owes O'Brien more than a hundred dollars and offers

O'Brien two hundred. O'Brien refuses the money, but the next morning he finds four fifty-dollar bills in an envelope tacked to his door. Looking back on this time in his life, O'Brien marvels at his innocence. He invites us to reflect with him, to pretend that we're watching an old home movie of O'Brien, tan and fit, wearing faded blue jeans and a white polo shirt, sitting on Elroy's dock, and thinking about writing an apologetic letter to his parents.

On O'Brien's last full day at the Tip Top Lodge, Elroy takes him fishing on the Rainy River. During the voyage it occurs to O'Brien that they must have stopped in Canadian territory—soon after, Elroy stops the boat. O'Brien stares at the shoreline of Canada, twenty yards ahead of him, and wonders what to do. Elroy pretends not to notice as O'Brien bursts into tears. O'Brien tells himself he will run to Canada, but he silently concludes that he will go to war because he is embarrassed not to. Elroy pulls in his line and turns the boat back toward Minnesota. The next morning, O'Brien washes the breakfast dishes, leaves the two hundred dollars on the kitchen counter, and drives south to his home. He then goes off to war.

ANALYSIS

"On the Rainy River" is an exploration of the role of shame in war. The story develops the theme of embarrassment as a motivating factor, first introduced by Jimmy Cross in "The Things They Carried" and "Love." Just as Jimmy Cross feels guilty about Ted Lavender's death, O'Brien feels guilty about going to Vietnam against his principles. He questions his own motives, and in this story he returns to the genesis of his decision in order to examine with us the specifics of cause and effect.

Ironically, despite its specific details and its preoccupation with reality, "On the Rainy River" is the story most easily identifiable as fiction. The real Tim O'Brien did indeed struggle with his decision to heed his draft notice, but he never actually ran to the Canadian border, and he never stayed at the Tip Top Lodge. Still, as he states explicitly later in the work, the point of a story like this one is not to deliver true facts exactly as they happened but rather to use facts and details in order to give an accurate account of the feelings behind a given situation. Though the events in the story are not true, the story itself conveys an emotional truth.

By describing his personal history, O'Brien makes a broader comment on the confusion that soldiers experienced when the demands of their country and community conflicted with the demands of their princples and conscience. O'Brien's description of his moral dilemma about going to Vietnam illustrates how the war was fought by soldiers who were often reluctant and conflicted. In the context of the collection's later stories, "On the Rainy River" weighs the guilt of avoiding the draft against the guilt of committing atrocities against other humans. Though it seems obvious that killing is more ethically reprehensible than draft-dodging, O'Brien's story explains how his largely uninformed community nonetheless wields a moral clout that overpowers his own opposition to the war.

This story references one of the recurring ideas in *The Things They Carried*: that war twists moral structures and makes it impossible to take a morally clear course of action. Joseph Heller's World War II novel *Catch-22* also addresses the twisted morality of war by describing a situation, called a "catch-22," in which a problem's only solution is impossible because of some characteristic of the problem. O'Brien is trapped in a catch-22 because the only way that he can avoid guilt is by taking a course of action that will make him feel guilty. If he goes to war, he will feel guilty for ignoring his own objection to United States involvement in Vietnam, but the only way to avoid this guilt involves incurring the disapproval of his community—which will cause him to feel guilt and shame. In *The Things They Carried*, O'Brien shows how soldiers experience catch-22s both during the war and in the time surrounding it.

The bald, shrunken, silent Elroy Berdahl is a father figure for the narrator. Although the two do not explicitly discuss O'Brien's dilemma, Elroy forces O'Brien to shake himself out of complacent confusion. But Berdahl's presence isn't sharp or invasive. Rather, his effect is that of a mirror—saying nothing, expecting nothing, perhaps not even knowing the situation at hand, he leads O'Brien to the river and forces him to confront Canada and the prospect of freedom from the draft sitting on the other side. O'Brien is compelled into action, not because Elroy forces him, but rather because the old man leads him to the river, where the necessity of making a choice once and for all becomes clear to O'Brien.

O'Brien's narrative reveals that he feels the need to justify and explain his decision to us, his readers, by putting us in the position of ethical judges of his actions. O'Brien's description of himself as a naïve, impressionable youth is part of a defense of himself and of his actions. Although his blunt questioning of "What would you do?" and "Would you cry, as I did?" forces us to recognize the difficulty of his position, it also invites us to evaluate the validity of his course of action. Later in the work, O'Brien illustrates the ==power of war to transform== an individual by showing his ==own transformation== from ==young and impressionable to disillusioned and uninspired==. Here, he compares the act of remembering his young, naïve self to watching an old home movie, and this metaphor makes us the audience of this movie and forces us to take a more active role in considering O'Brien.

"Enemies" & "Friends"

Summary: "Enemies"
One morning on patrol Dave Jensen and Lee Strunk get into a fistfight over a missing jackknife that Jensen thinks Strunk has stolen. Jensen breaks Strunk's nose, hitting him repeatedly and without mercy. Afterward, Jensen is nervous that Strunk will try to get revenge and pays special attention to Strunk's whereabouts. Finally, crazed by apprehension, Jensen fires his gun into the air and calls out Strunk's name. Later that night, he borrows a pistol and uses it to break his own nose in order to even the score. The next morning, Strunk is amused by the news, admitting that he *did* steal Jensen's jackknife.

Summary: "Friends"
Dave Jensen and Lee Strunk learn to trust each other. They resolve that if one gets seriously wounded, the other will kill him to put him out of his misery. In October, Strunk's lower leg gets blown off by a mortar round. Jensen kneels at his side and Strunk repeatedly begs not to be killed. Strunk is loaded into a helicopter, and later Jensen is relieved to learn that Strunk didn't survive the trip.

Analysis: "Enemies" & "Friends"
In these two brief stories, the pressures of war distort social codes, causing two men on the same side to act violently toward one another for no real reason. O'Brien explains that this behavior results from the immaturity of Jensen and Strunk, and of the immaturity of grunts in general. Amid the chaotic war in Vietnam, soldiers often battled one another, to relieve the tension of waiting and because such close confines inspired contentious relationships.

In this story, social codes and contracts become arbitrary. In most societies, those who steal are punished by others in order to inspire guilt about, and fear of, committing wrongs. However, in "Enemies," the lack of an attempt by Jensen and Strunk to resolve their conflict using peaceful dialogue demonstrates that social contracts have begun to break down. While Jensen assumes that Strunk will inflict eye-for-an-eye revenge on him for breaking his nose, Strunk assumes Jensen was somewhat justified in his rash action and in the end Strunk feels that he's gotten what he deserved, since he did steal Jensen's jackknife. Strunk's acceptance of the matter and the relief Jensen takes in his exaggerated gesture of settling the score show that both men are willing to take responsibility for their actions. Unfortunately, with the breakdown of the social code, each is taking responsibility out of guilt rather than integrity.

The irony in these two stories is expressed by their titles. At the beginning of "Enemies," Jensen and Strunk are violently opposed to one another although they are fighting on the same side of a brutal war. At the end of "Friends," Jensen is relieved rather than aggrieved to learn of Strunk's death, although the two are supposed to be friends. These titles emphasize a wartime distortion of the notion of friendship, especially when compared with the notion of fidelity and promises. Jensen's relief at Strunk's death signals that he operates under a strict code of right and wrong, putting more stock in fidelity and promises than in friendship. Just as he assumes, in "Enemies," that he has broken a social code by wronging Strunk and must therefore feel bad, so too in "Friends" does he feel he has broken a social code by not honoring the terms of his pact with Strunk, even though Strunk is the one who waves off the pact.

O'Brien contends that war is a time when fantasies are shattered and notions of honor are rendered obsolete in the frightening face of death. When Jensen and Strunk make their pact, they are thinking of both grave injury and death as abstract, distant things, remnants of their notions of heroism from before the war, that have yet to become real because of their relative inexperience with death since their arrival. But when Strunk is actually injured, he immediately wants to rescind the agreement made in a time when the prospect of its being enacted seemed unlikely. Being alive and injured is better than being dead, he realizes. As Strunk begs for his life, Jensen is forced to grant an escape clause to the pact. Still, although Jensen doesn't take action to kill Strunk, the relief he feels upon hearing of Strunk's death suggests he believes that there was a right—honoring the pact—and a wrong—honoring Strunk's revised wishes—in this situation.

"How to Tell a True War Story"

Summary

O'Brien prefaces this story by saying that it is true. A week after his friend is killed, Rat Kiley writes a letter to the friend's sister, explaining what a hero her brother was and how much he loved him. Two months pass, and the sister never writes back. Kiley, frustrated, spits and calls the sister a "dumb cooze." O'Brien insists that a true war story is not moral and tells us not to believe a story that seems moral. He uses Kiley's actions as an example of the amorality of war stories. O'Brien reveals that Kiley's friend's name was Curt Lemon and that he died while playfully tossing a smoke grenade with Rat Kiley, in the shade of some trees. Lemon stepped into the sunlight and onto a rigged mortar round.

O'Brien says sometimes a true war story cannot be believed because some of the most unbearable parts are true, while some of the normal parts are not. Sometimes, he says, a true war story is impossible to tell. He describes a story that Mitchell Sanders tells. Sanders recounts the experience of a troop that goes into the mountains on a listening post operation. He says that after a few days, the men hear strange echoes and music—chimes and xylophones—and become frightened. One night, the men hear voices and noises that sound like a cocktail party. After a while they hear singing and chanting, as well as talking monkeys and trees. They order air strikes and they burn and shoot down everything they can find. Still, in the morning, they hear the noises. So they pack up their gear and head down the mountain, where their colonel asks them what they heard. They have no answer.

The day after he tells this story, Mitchell approaches O'Brien and confesses that some parts were invented. O'Brien asks him what the moral of the story is and, listening to the quiet, Sanders says the quiet is the moral. O'Brien says the moral of a true war story, like the thread that makes a cloth, cannot be separated from the story itself. A true war story cannot be made general or abstract, he says. The significance of the story is whether or not you believe it in your stomach. Heeding his own advice, he relays the story of Curt Lemon's death in a few, brief vignettes. He explains that the platoon crossed a muddy river and on the third day Lemon was killed and Kiley lost his best friend. Later that day, higher in the mountains, Kiley shot a Viet Cong water buffalo repeatedly—though the animal was destroyed and bleeding, it remained alive. Finally Kiowa and Sanders picked up the buffalo and dumped it in the village well.

O'Brien expounds on his problem by making a generalization. He says that though war is hell, it is also many other contradictory things. He explains the mysterious feeling of being alive that follows a firefight. He agrees with Sanders's story of the men who hear things in the jungle—war is ambiguous, he says. For this reason, in a true war story, nothing is absolutely true. O'Brien remembers how Lemon died. Lemon was smiling and talking to Kiley one second and was blown into a tree the next. Jensen and O'Brien were ordered to climb the tree to retrieve Lemon's body, and Jensen sang "Lemon Tree" as they threw down the body parts.

A true war story can be identified by the questions one asks afterward, O'Brien says. He says that in the story of a man who jumps on a grenade to save his three friends, the truth of the man's purpose makes a difference. He says that sometimes the truest war stories never happened and tells a story of the same four men—one jumps on a grenade to take the blast, and all four die anyway. Before they die, though, one of the dead turns to the man who jumped on the grenade and asks him why he jumped. The already-dead jumper says, "Story of my life, man."

Thinking of Curt Lemon, O'Brien concludes he must have thought the sunlight was killing him. O'Brien wishes he could get the story right—the way the sunlight seemed to gather Lemon and carry him up in the air—so that we could believe what Lemon must have seen as his final truth.

O'Brien says that when he tells this story, a woman invariably approaches him and tells him that she liked it but it made her sad, and that O'Brien should find new stories to tell. O'Brien wishes he could tell the woman that the story he told wasn't a war story but a love story. He concludes that all he can do is continue telling it, making up more things in order give greater truth to the story.

Analysis

"How to Tell a True War Story" examines the complex relationship between the war experience and storytelling. It is told half from O'Brien's role as a soldier, as a reprise of several old Vietnam stories, and half from his role as a storyteller, as a discourse on the art of storytelling. O'Brien's narrative shows that a storyteller has the power to shape his or her listeners' experiences and opinions. Much in the same way that the war distorts the soldier's perceptions of right and wrong, O'Brien's story distorts our perceptions of beauty and ugliness. O'Brien tells Curt Lemon's death as a love story. Despite its gruesomeness, evident by O'Brien's graphic recounting of the situation, he describes the scene as beautiful, focusing on the sunlight rather than the carnage. Blood and carnage are never even discussed, not even as O'Brien and Dave Jensen are forced to shimmy up the tree in order to throw down Curt Lemon's body parts. The way O'Brien describes this action, and the death in general, is unspecific and detached. His storytelling functions as a salve that allows him to deal with the complexity of the war experience, so much even as to turn the story of Curt Lemon from a war story to a love story.

A true war story, O'Brien explains, has an absolute allegiance to obscenity and evil that renders commonly held storytelling notions of courage and pride obsolete. When we learn that Rat Kiley sends a letter to Curt Lemon's sister, extolling the virtues of his fellow soldier after his death, we expect the death and the story to have a positive, heartwarming outcome. The essence of the true war story lies in the reality of the situation: the sister does not respond, and Kiley reacts immaturely. This irony makes sense, O'Brien contends, both because Kiley is young and because he has been exposed to such unspeakable things. He calls the sister a "dumb cooze" not because he is a misogynist but because it is his way of negotiating anger. Blame must be assigned, Kiley rationalizes in his anger, and O'Brien sees the truth in Kiley's emotions. A true war story is not about courage and heroism but about the reality of misplaced anger and the inability of soldiers to deal effectively with their feelings about a horrible experience.

Although all members of the Alpha Company are effectively soldiers turned storytellers, O'Brien and Sanders take their role as storytellers more seriously than the rest. Ironically, Sanders's most vehement piece of advice—to get out of the way and to let the story tell itself—is one that both he and O'Brien ignore. When he inserts himself into his story about the soldiers who hear voices, Sanders gets in the way, with his comments and clarifications, where he might have let the image of the men speak for itself. This contradiction proves that there are no truths to storytelling, even and especially in true war stories.

Sanders's advice points out that even in the case of an unreliable narrator, the truest part of a true war story is the listener's visceral reaction to the details. O'Brien insists the story is absolutely true, but then, after telling it, in a more general discussion of storytelling, insists that it's difficult to separate what happened from what seemed to happen. The only conclusion we can arrive at is that truth in a true war story is irrelevant. O'Brien is so explicit as to say "war is hell," but that simple statement has little impact because it is so general and clichéd. Truth is what "makes the stomach believe," like the image of Rat Kiley torturing a buffalo because he cannot sit with his emotions about Curt Lemon's death. The image of this suffering Viet Cong buffalo that refuses to die is a far more vivid testament to war than a hollow cry of "war is hell."

"The Dentist"

Summary
O'Brien says that mourning Curt Lemon was difficult for him because he didn't know him well, but in order to avoid getting sentimental, he tells a brief Curt Lemon story. In February, the men are at work in an area of operations along the South China Sea. One day, an Army dentist is flown in to check the men's teeth. As the platoon sits, waiting to be checked one by one, Curt Lemon begins to tense up. Finally, he admits that in high school he had some bad experiences with dentists. He says that no one messes with his teeth, and that when he's called, he'll refuse to go in. However, a few moments later, when the dentist calls him, Lemon rises and goes into the tent. He faints before the dentist can even lay a finger on him.

Later that night he creeps back to the dental tent and insists that he has a killer toothache. Though the dentist can't find any problem, Lemon demands his tooth be pulled. Finally, the dentist, shrugging, gives him a shot and yanks the perfectly good tooth out, to Lemon's delight.

Analysis
Curt Lemon's character offers an unusual take on the idea of bravado within war. He has an obvious need to demonstrate his capacity to endure suffering and to act bravely in the face of adversity. He, like several of the men, has a clear notion of what bravery is, garnered from popular culture. He experiences discomfort for the sake of pride and for the assurance that he has acted like a man. In the morning, when he reveals that the dentist has pulled his tooth, he is

proud, having defeated his prior nervous reaction—fainting—with an obvious display of manliness. But the threat that Lemon faces is not a real one; nothing is wrong with his teeth. The challenge that he confronts with bravado is entirely psychological. As a result, this episode demonstrates the absurdity of conventional bravado.

Before his death, Curt Lemon is the work's most comic character. Despite his seemingly ridiculous actions, we can identify with Lemon's need to prove himself for the sake of proving himself. He is a young, frightened man whose notions of pain are, at this point, reserved to the dentist's chair. The irony of the story is that shortly after he gets up the courage to have a tooth pulled in order to reassure himself of his bravery, he is killed while playing catch with a grenade. His death is ridiculous and points out the uselessness of bravery. The irony of Lemon's character is that Lemon so abjectly fears something as generally harmless as a dentist's visit and doesn't give a second thought to the potential harm of playing with a grenade.

The truth O'Brien attempts to illustrate in "The Dentist" is that physical suffering is sometimes easier to bear than mental anguish. For the soldiers in Vietnam, the unknown was often their greatest enemy. Lemon wants to get his pain out of the way—in part to save face in front of his fellow soldiers for fainting and in part to get used to the feeling of suffering. By actually experiencing and becoming familiar with pain, he eases his mind of the anxiety of not knowing what such pain might feel like. O'Brien portrays such seemingly small triumphs as necessary victories amid the chaos and senselessness of war.

"Sweetheart of the Song Tra Bong"

Summary

O'Brien says the most enduring Vietnam stories are those that are between the absolutely unbelievable and the mundane. Rat Kiley, who has a reputation for exaggeration, tells a story of his first assignment in the mountains of Chu Lai, in a protected and isolated area where he ran an aid station with eight other men near a river called the Song Tra Bong. One day, Eddie Diamond, the highest ranking man in his company and a pleasure-seeker, jokingly suggests that the area is so unguarded and seemingly safe that you could even bring a girl to the camp there. A younger medic, Mark Fossie, seems interested in the idea and goes off to write a letter. Six weeks later, his elementary school sweetheart, Mary Anne Bell, arrives, carried in by helicopter with a resupply shipment. Fossie explains that getting her to camp was difficult but not impossible and for the next two weeks, they carry on like school children. Mary Anne is curious and a fast learner—she picks up some Vietnamese and learns how to cook. When four casualties come in, she isn't afraid to tend to them, learning how to repair arteries and shoot morphine. She drops her fussy feminine habits and cuts her hair short.

After a while, Fossie suggests that Mary Anne think about going home, but she argues that she is content staying. She makes plans to travel before she and Fossie marry. She begins coming home later and a few times not at all. One night she is missing, and when Fossie goes out looking, he discovers that she has been out the entire night on an ambush, where she refused to carry a gun. The next morning, Fossie and Mary Anne exchange words and seem to have reached a new understanding. They become officially engaged and discuss wedding plans in the mess hall, but over the next several nights it becomes clear that there is a strain on their relationship. Fossie makes arrangements to send her home but Mary Anne is not pleased with the prospect—she becomes withdrawn, and she eventually disappears.

Mary Anne returns three weeks later, but she doesn't even stop at her fiancé's bunk—she goes straight to the Special Forces hut. The next morning, Fossie stations himself outside the Special Forces area, where he waits until after midnight. When Kiley and Eddie Diamond go to check on Fossie, he says he can hear Mary Anne singing. He lunges forward into the hut, and the two others follow. Inside they see dozens of candles burning and hear tribal music. On a post near the back of the bunk is the head of a leopard—its skin dangles from the rafters. When Fossie finally sees Mary Anne she is in the same outfit—pink sweater, white blouse, cotton skirt—that she was wearing when she arrived weeks before. But when he approaches her, he sees a necklace made of human tongues around her neck. She insists to Fossie that what she is doing isn't bad and that he, in his sheltered camp, doesn't understand Vietnam.

Kiley says that he never knew what happened with Mary Anne because three or four days later he received orders to join the Alpha Company. But he confesses that he loved Mary Anne—that everyone did. Two months after he left, when he ran into Eddie Diamond, he learned that Mary Anne delighted in night patrols and in the fire. She had crossed to the other side and had become part of the land.

Analysis

In this story, O'Brien paints a highly stylized version of Vietnam as a world that profoundly affects the foreign Americans who inhabit it. He portrays a stark difference between the native world of Vietnam and the world of the Americans. Mary Anne Bell fully embraces Vietnamese culture, while Mark Fossie ignores it. The difference between their experiences sets up a world in which the separate cultures are completely foreign to, and incompatible with, each other. O'Brien does not suggest that one can assimilate elements of each culture into a comfortabe mix. Rather, the characters must choose a single cultural identity.

"Sweetheart of the Song Tra Bong" refutes the idea of women as one-dimensional beings who serve only to offer comfort to men. Fossie assumes that if he brings Mary Anne over to the relatively comfortable quarters he and his men keep, he will gain her comfort and companionship and she will remain unaffected by her surroundings. This fantasy is immediately shattered as Mary Anne is instantly curious about the things surrounding her—from the language and the locals to the ammunition and the procedures and finally the nature of war itself. The irony of this story is that Mary Anne's new reality agrees with her, perhaps more than her conventional life. She is enlivened and empowered by war: its influence prompts her to make plans for future travel and to attempt to steer her path away from the life she earlier considered desirable. Ironically, although her soldier boyfriend brings her over to be a comfort while he is in the midst of war, in the end, Mary Anne's conversion makes her hungrier for adventure than he is.

Fossie tries to understand Mary Anne by transfering the values and power structure of their native Cleveland Heights to Vietnam, but the foreign culture renders his method of interpreting her behavior meaningless. Mary Anne herself becomes a component of the foreign Vietnam, inexplicable to Fossie, who remains an outsider. Like Kurtz in Joseph Conrad's *Heart of Darkness,* Mary Anne enters the wild, uncivilized jungle and becomes irrevocably enthralled by the forbidding world so different from her own. Whereas Kurtz finds himself reborn deep in Africa, Mary Anne falls in love with Vietnam, embracing the jungle, which is mysterious to the soldiers. She negotiates the uncertainty of war differently than Fossie and the others. Her feeling that she has nothing to lose saves further oppression back in Ohio and allows her to avoid a life of inevitabilities, and she joins the Green Berets to break out of a prison of gender norms.

Mary Anne's tongue necklace represents her desire to be a part of Vietnamese culture. The tongues symbolize consumption, both literal and figurative. Mary Anne is willing to be consumed by the jungle and to become a consumer of Vietnamese culture. Embraced by the tongues and surrounded by other tribal symbols, Mary Anne defends herself against Fossie's horror and condemnation. She makes a distinction between those like Fossie and his fellow soldiers who are present in Vietnam because they have to be and those like herself and her newfound friends who have a greater respect for the land. She has grown fearless and accepting, because she has resigned herself to the fact that Vietnam will consume her.

"Stockings"

Summary

O'Brien relates that on ambushes, and sometimes in bed, Henry Dobbins wears his girlfriend's pantyhose around his neck. Superstitions are prevalent in Vietnam, and the pantyhose are Dobbins's good luck charm. With the pantyhose around his neck, Dobbins survives tripping over a land mine, and a week later he survives a firefight. In October, Dobbins's girlfriend dumps him. Despite the pain of the rejection, he ties the pantyhose around his neck, remarking that the magic hasn't been lost.

Analysis

"Stockings" and "Sweetheart of the Song Tra Bong" are thematically opposed in their treatment of the relationship between soldiers and women. While "Sweetheart of the Song Tra Bong" challenges the idea that manifestations of femininity serve as comforting reminders of home, "Stockings" enforces it. The story affirms Henry Dobbins's notion that his girlfriend's stockings, which he ties around his neck, keep him from harm. At the same time, however, it emphasizes that this tactic is, in the end, nothing but superstition. Dobbins originally rationalizes wearing the stockings because their smell and feel remind him of his girlfriend and of a safer world away from Vietnam. But even after their breakup, he continues to wear the stockings, contending that their special, protective power has not been destroyed. Though his ex-girlfriend no longer offers herself as a source of comfort to him, he continues to perceive her as one.

O'Brien shows how American soldiers order their experience by superstition rather than by rationality. To the soldiers in Vietnam, superstition became a kind of religion, a faith that might save them individually from the ironic twists of fate omnipresent in the mysterious jungle. Dobbins's girlfriend comes to exist for him in the realm of superstition; she becomes more of an imagined symbol than a real person. When she breaks up with Dobbins through a letter, her abandonment has no bearing on the protective power of the mystical stockings, since it is what she represents rather than who she is that endows them with their significance.

O'Brien doesn't use a satirical or ridiculing tone when describing Dobbins and his belief, despite its seeming inconsistency and implausibility. Indeed, in the end, Dobbins does survive the war, perhaps because the stockings keep him motivated to survive by giving him a reminder of home. In any case, the belief in the power of the stockings is more important than the objective truth of their power. Because the stockings cushion Dobbins from reality, they improve his psychological condition. With "Stockings," O'Brien contends that rationally thinking men can be made to think irrationally in order to preserve their well-being.

"Church"

Summary
One afternoon, the platoon comes across an abandoned pagoda that seems to function as a church. Every day during the men's stay there, which lasts more than a week, two monks bring them water and other goods. One day, while the monks clean and oil Dobbins's M-60 machine gun, Dobbins says that though he isn't a religious man and wouldn't enjoy taking part in the sermons, he might like to join the church because he would enjoy interacting with people. Kiowa says that although he carries a Bible everywhere because he was raised to, he wouldn't enjoy being a preacher. He does say, though, that he enjoys being in a church. When the monks finish cleaning the gun, Dobbins wipes off the excess oil and hands them each a can of peaches and a chocolate bar. Making a washing motion with his hands, he says that all one can do is be nice to them.

Analysis

The abandoned pagoda in this story is a microcosm of American-Vietnamese relations. Dobbins and Kiowa's questioning of their presence in this makeshift church stands in for Americans' questioning of their army's presence in Vietnam. When the soldiers happen upon the church, they discover that it is occupied by well-intentioned monks who welcome them by offering favors. The irony in the story is that frequently during the Vietnam War, American soldiers committed atrocities against innocent civilians. Dobbins's comment that "[a]ll you can do is be nice" is made ironic by his gesture of washing his hands. Although this action can be construed as a sign of respect for the monks, who have called Dobbins "Good soldier Jesus," it also alludes to the New Testament account of Pontius Pilate's symbolic washing of his hands after Jesus Christ was sentenced to be crucified. Keeping with the church-as-Vietnam symbolism, the monks perhaps do not know what sort of destruction the American soldiers might inflict.

In "Church," O'Brien uses Kiowa as a foil—a character whose actions or emotions contrast with and thereby accentuate those of another character—for Dobbins. Kiowa's Native American thoughtfulness contrasts with Henry Dobbins's sweeping American ambition. While Kiowa is the more religious of the two men, he can't conceive of wanting to take a leadership role in church. For him, religion is as close to his heart as the New Testament he carries with him through the jungles of Vietnam. He says he can't imagine wanting to preach because for him, unlike Dobbins, religion is not about demonstration or even about participation—it is about inward reflection and the power of belief.

Although both Dobbins and Kiowa agree that setting up camp inside a church is wrong, the two men are trapped by the inevitability of their situations. Dobbins tries to improve the situation by giving the monks a tin of peaches and some chocolate—this small gesture lends a touch of humanity to offset the impersonal and selfish invasion of the monks' place of worship. Similarly, later, in the story "Style," Dobbins admonishes Azar for poking fun at a Vietnamese girl's suffering. Perhaps believing that his presence in the war is wrong, he operates under the belief that the one small thing he might do in this impossible situation is to "be nice" to those who deserve no harm.

"The Man I Killed"

> *He was a slim, dead, almost dainty young man of about twenty.* (See QUOTATIONS, p. 68)

Summary

"The Man I Killed" begins with a list of physical attributes and possible characteristics of the man whom O'Brien killed with a grenade in My Khe. O'Brien describes the wounds that he inflicted. The man's jaw was in his throat, he says, and his upper lip and teeth were missing. One eye was shut, and the other looked like a star-shaped hole. O'Brien imagines that the man he killed was born in 1946 and that his parents were farmers; that he was neither a Communist nor a fighter and that he hoped the Americans would go away.

O'Brien describes the reaction of his platoon-mates—insensitive Azar compares the young man to oatmeal, Shredded Wheat, and Rice Krispies, while Kiowa rationalizes O'Brien's actions and urges him to take his time coming to terms with the death. All the while, O'Brien reflects on the boy's life, cut short. He looks at the boy's sunken chest and delicate fingers and wonders if he was a scholar. He imagines that the other boys at school might have teased this boy because he may have had a woman's walk and a love for mathematics. A butterfly lands on the corpse's cheek, which causes O'Brien to notice the undamaged nose. Despite Kiowa's urging to pull himself together, to talk about it, and to stop staring at the body, O'Brien cannot do so. Kiowa confesses that maybe he doesn't understand what O'Brien is going through, but he rationalizes that the young man was carrying a weapon and that they are fighting a war. He asks if O'Brien would rather trade places with him. O'Brien doesn't respond to Kiowa.

O'Brien notices that the young man's head is lying by tiny blue flowers and that his cheek is peeled back in three ragged strips. He imagines that the boy began studying at the university in Saigon in 1964, that he avoided politics and favored calculus. He notices that the butterfly has disappeared. Kiowa bends down to search the body, taking the young man's personal affects, including a picture of a young woman standing in front of a motorcycle. He rationalizes that if O'Brien had not killed him, one of the other men surely would have. But O'Brien says nothing, even after Kiowa insists the company will move out in five minutes' time. When that time has passed, Kiowa covers the body and says O'Brien looks like he might be feeling better. He urges him again to talk, but all O'Brien can think of is the boy's daintiness and his eye that looks like a star-shaped hole.

Analysis

In "The Man I Killed" O'Brien's guilt has him so fixated on the life of his victim that his own presence in the story—as protagonist and narrator—fades to the back. Since he doesn't use the first person to explain his guilt and confusion, he negotiates his feelings by operating in fantasy—by imagining an entire life for his victim, from his boyhood and his family to his feeling about the war and about the Americans. His guilt almost takes on its own rhythm in the repetition of ideas, phrases, and observations. Some of the ideas here, especially the notion of the victim being a "slim, young, dainty man," help emphasize O'Brien's fixation on the effects of his action. At the same time, his focus on these physical characteristics, rather than on his own feelings, betrays his attempt to keep some distance in order to dull the pain.

Because O'Brien tells this story from the perspective of the protagonist rather than the narrator, there is no narrative commentary on the protagonist's action, and we can only infer what O'Brien is feeling. He conveys an implicit silence surrounding death in Vietnam that first becomes evident with Ted Lavender's death. After Lavender's death, men like Kiowa and Norman Bowker struggle to find words and perspective on the tragedy. Similarly, all O'Brien can remember of the day of Curt Lemon's death is the sunlight. In "The Man I Killed," O'Brien employs the same distancing tactics but pushes them to an extreme, offering no insight into the way he feels. In the action is the implicit contention that by focusing on other aspects of the death, like the sunlight or, in the case of the man O'Brien killed, his physical features and the flowers growing on the road, he finds safety from guilt.

The ineffective comments and attempted consolations of O'Brien's fellow soldiers and the palpable silence demonstrate that nothing can erase the stark facts of life and death. Azar's tasteless offers of congratulations to O'Brien and comparisons of the dead boy to cereal ignore the painful guilt that O'Brien feels. The kinder Kiowa is patient with O'Brien's pain, but he knows that he can identify with O'Brien only to a certain degree. Ultimately, anyhow, Kiowa seems more interested in trying to convince O'Brien that the killing is no big deal than in helping him work through his emotions. In between the remarks from the others, O'Brien sits in the inevitable silence of Vietnam—a stillness that forces one to confront the realities of war.

O'Brien both consoles and tortures himself by indulging in a fantasy that he shares several characteristics with the man he killed. Ironically, the similarity that he imagines is a consolation for him, despite the implication that he has killed a replica of himself. By relating to his victim in this way, O'Brien grapples with and tries to understand the arbitrariness of his own mortality. He imagines that like himself, the man is a student who, in the presence of his family, pretended to look forward to doing his patriotic duty. By doing so he in effect imagines his own death by putting himself in the Vietnamese soldier's shoes. But with the same fantasy, he also tortures himself, by imagining exactly why the man's death might be such a horrible tragedy. O'Brien feeds his guilt by imagining that the man he killed was in the prime of his life. By imagining that the man he killed wrote romantic poems in his journal and had fallen in love with a classmate whom he married before he enlisted as a common rifleman, O'Brien can more easily identify with his victim and understand the terrible nature of the killing.

O'Brien illustrates the ambiguity and complexity of Vietnam by alternating explicit references to beauty and gore. The butterfly and the tiny blue flowers he mentions show the mystery and suddenness of death in the face of pristine natural phenomena. O'Brien's observations of his victim lying on the side of the road—his jaw in his throat and his upper lip gone—emphasize the unnaturalness of war amid nature. The contrast of images is an incredibly ironic one that suggests the tragedy of death amid so much beauty. However, the presence of the butterfly and the tiny blue flowers also suggests that life goes on even despite such unspeakable tragedy. After O'Brien killed the Vietnamese soldier, the flowers didn't shrivel up, and the butterfly didn't fly away. They stayed and found their home around the tragedy. In this way, like the story of Curt Lemon's death, "The Man I Killed" is a story about the beauty of life rather than the gruesomeness of death.

"Ambush"

Summary

More than twenty years after the end of the war, O'Brien's daughter Kathleen asks O'Brien if he has ever killed anyone. She contends that he can't help himself from obsessively writing war stories because he killed someone. O'Brien, however, insists that he has never killed anyone. Reflecting on his lie, O'Brien pretends Kathleen is an adult and imagines that he might tell her the entire story of My Khe.

O'Brien recounts that in the middle of the night, the platoon, separated into two-man teams, moved into the ambush site outside My Khe. O'Brien, teamed up with Kiowa, noticed dawn breaking slowly, in slivers. As Kiowa slept, O'Brien, fighting off mosquitoes, saw a young soldier wearing an ammunition belt coming out of the fog. The only reality O'Brien could feel was the sour nervousness in his stomach, and without thinking, he pulled the key in the grenade before he realized what he was doing. When the grenade bounced, the young man dropped his weapon and began to run. He then hesitated and tried to cover his head—only then did O'Brien realize that the man was about to die. The grenade went off and the man fell on his back, his sandals blown off.

O'Brien grapples with his guilt. He insists that the situation was not one of life and death, and that had he not pulled the pin in the grenade, the man would have passed by. Kiowa contended that the young man would have died anyway. O'Brien states that none of it mattered. Even now, twenty years later, he still hasn't finished sorting it out. He says that he sees the young man coming through the fog sometimes when he's reading the newspaper or sitting alone. He imagines the young man walking up the trail, passing him, smiling at a secret thought and continuing on his way.

Analysis

O'Brien recounts this story in the first person, using a thorough, almost historical method of storytelling. Whereas in "The Man I Killed" O'Brien avoids directly confronting the boy's death—the word "I" is never used by the narrator in the story—in "Ambush" he tries to be clinical about it. Part of the reason for this difference is this story's intended audience, O'Brien's daughter Kathleen. In relaying this experience to us and in imagining he might one day tell his daughter so she understands him, O'Brien leaves out no detail, so that the taste and feeling and sense of the day he killed a man outside of My Khe is entirely intact. In this way, "Ambush" differs greatly from "The Man I Killed." Though its intact narrative, complete with observations, is constructed nominally for the benefit of Kathleen, "Ambush" is definitely for O'Brien's sake as well. Unlike "The Man I Killed," which comes from a place much more immediate, "Ambush" is marked by clear narrative control and a strong sense of perspective.

"The Man I Killed" sets up ideas that are addressed in "Ambush," just as "The Things They Carried" sets up ideas that are addressed in "Love." The refrains of "The Man I Killed," such as "he was a short, slender man of about twenty," are constant, adding to the continuity of the storytelling. Unlike "The Man I Killed," which seems to take place in real time, "Ambush" is already a memory story—one with perspective, history, and a sense of life's continuation. As such, O'Brien uses his narrative to clear up some of the questions that we might have about the somewhat ambiguous version of the story in "The Man I Killed." But O'Brien's memory is crystal clear. He remembers how he lobbed the grenade and that it seemed to freeze in the air for a moment, perhaps indicating his momentary regret even before the explosion detonated. He has a clear vision of the man's actual death that he probably could not have articulated so close to the occurrence. O'Brien's simile about the man seeming to jerk upward, as though pulled by invisible wires, suggests that the actions of the men in Vietnam were not entirely voluntary. They were propelled by another power outside of them—the power of guilt and responsibility and impulse and regret.

"Style"

Summary

Though most of her village has burned to the ground and her family has been burned to death by the American soldiers, a Vietnamese girl of fourteen dances through the wreckage. The men of the platoon cannot understand why she is dancing. Azar contends that the dance is a strange ritual, but Dobbins insists that the girl probably just likes to dance.

Later that night, Azar mocks the girl's dancing by jumping and spinning, putting his hands against his ears and then making an erotic motion with his hips. Dobbins grabs Azar from behind, carries him over to the mouth of a well, and threatens to dump him in if he doesn't dance properly.

Analysis

"Style," like "Church," concerns the contrast and ambiguity of good intentions and ill intentions. In this story, Henry Dobbins rebukes Azar for his insensitivity by hanging him over the mouth of a well. Yet the moral ambiguity of the story remains—a few moments earlier, Dobbins helps destroy an entire village. He is hardly occupying a moral high ground. Even so, Dobbins, more than Azar, retains some moral beliefs. In this case, he thinks it cruel to mock those who have been tortured—even though he is partly responsible for this torture.

The Vietnamese girl's dancing despite the lack of music makes clear an innate human ability to find pleasure even during moments of abject horror. Henry Dobbins, like many soldiers, and like the "typical American" to whom O'Brien compares him in "Church," doesn't want to explore the human side of the Vietnamese because he doesn't want to confront the guilt of inflicting pain on them. Their plight seems irrelevant to his mission, and by keeping the girl at enough of a distance that she remains a phenomenon rather than a real person profoundly affected by their actions, the soldiers can continue on their mission with a relatively clear conscience. Nevertheless, when Azar mocks the girl's dancing and wonders at her attempt to find joy or distraction from the horrors surrounding her, Dobbins discourages him. He may think the girl's dancing a strange reaction to such horror, but he also thinks the soldiers owe some small respect to the people they have so irrevocably harmed.

All of the men are too caught up in the situation to realize that the girl's dancing is similar to Dobbins's carrying his girlfriend's stockings around his neck—both seemingly nonsensical actions serve as a salve to the wounds of the war. But just as Dobbins's stockings cannot actually deflect a bullet or a round of mortar, the girl's dancing cannot bring back her family, her village, or life as she knew it before the war.

"Speaking of Courage"

Summary

After the war, Norman Bowker returns to Iowa. On the Fourth of July, as he drives his father's big Chevrolet around the lake, he realizes that he has nowhere to go. He reminisces about his high school girlfiend, Sally Kramer, who is now married. He thinks about his friend Max Arnold, who drowned in the lake. He thinks also of his father, whose greatest hope, that Norman would bring home medals from Vietnam, was satisfied. Norman won seven medals in Vietnam, including the Combat Infantryman's Badge, the Air Medal, the Army Commendation Medal, the Bronze Star, and the Purple Heart. He thinks about his father's pride in those badges and then recalls how he almost won the Silver Star but blew his chance. He drives around the town again and again, flicks on the radio, orders a hamburger at the A&W, and imagines telling his father the story of the way he almost won the Silver Star, when the banks of the Song Tra Bong overflowed.

The night the platoon settled in a field along the river, a group of Vietnamese women ran out to discourage them, but Lieutenant Jimmy Cross shooed them away. When they set up camp, they noticed a sour, fishlike smell. Finally, someone concluded that they had set up camp in a sewage field. Meanwhile, the rain poured down, and the earth bubbled with the heat and the excess moisture. Suddenly, rounds of mortar fell on the camp, and the field seemed to boil and explode. When the third round hit, Kiowa began screaming. Bowker saw Kiowa sink into the muck and grabbed him by the boot to pull him out. Yet Kiowa was lost, so Bowker let him go in order to save himself from sinking deeper into the muck.

Bowker wants to relate this memory to someone, but he doesn't have anyone to talk to. On his eleventh trip around the lake, he imagines telling his father the story and admitting that he did not act with the courage he hoped he might have. He imagines that his father might console him with the idea of the seven medals he *did* win. He parks his car and wades into the lake with his clothes on, submerging himself. He then stands up, folds his arms, and watches the holiday fireworks, remarking that they are pretty good, for a small town.

Analysis

Kiowa's death constitutes a climax in the series of stories. Because he is such a prominent character in the company's narrative, his death fundamentally changes the relationships among the company's individual members. Kiowa, a soft-spoken, peaceful Native American, serves as a foil for several of O'Brien's characters, including Henry Dobbins and Norman Bowker. His presence is strong but understated, and, by nature, he is a gentle and peaceful man. He discourages soldiers from excessive violence but also supports them through the difficult and inevitable decisions war forces them to make, especially, but not exclusively, when O'Brien kills a man outside My Khe. When Kiowa is killed suddenly and senselessly, all of the men are effected, specifically Norman Bowker, who worries that he has betrayed his friend.

The layers of narration in "Speaking of Courage" can be seen as a technique that the characters use to deal with survivor's guilt. In the story, Tim O'Brien tells the story of Norman Bowker thinking about how to tell the story of Kiowa's death. As readers, we are several steps removed from the death, both temporally, since the story of the death is told after the end of the war, and in terms of the narrative, since there are two separate characters between us and Kiowa's death. As a result, the story is as much about how these characters deal with the story of Kiowa's death as about Kiowa's death itself. Norman Bowker, for example, thinks that he was as brave as he thought he could have been, but that even that much bravery was not enough to save his friend. Such commentary provides us insight not only into Kiowa's death but also into Bowker's emotions.

"Speaking of Courage" explores the way that telling stories simultaneously recalls the pain of the war experience and allows soldiers to work through that pain after the war has ended. O'Brien and Bowker illustrate how speaking or not speaking about war experience affects characters. O'Brien deals with his memories and his guilt by writing stories about his fellow soldiers. At the same time that these stories make the experience of the war present for O'Brien again, they also distance him from the horrors. He writes in the past tense, differentiating between his present self and the self that fought in the war. Bowker, on the other hand, is unable to use the act of telling to negotiate the trauma of war. He drives around silently, with no one to talk to. Ironically, because he cannot speak about his war experience with anyone, he cannot leave it behind him. While O'Brien uses dialogue and communication to analyze and come to terms with his experience, Bowker's lack of an audience prevents him from arriving at a similar understanding.

Although we might expect that the atrocities of war would have rendered medals meaningless to Bowker, his return to his hometown reveals that the expectations of family and community members can determine what is meaningful as much as private experience can. As a result Bowker struggles with his father's feeling that medals are a relevant measure of personal worth and his own understanding that the medals are meaningless in the face of war's atrocities. O'Brien addresses this topic in "Spin" when he recalls Bowker rolling over in his bunk and wishing that his father would stop bothering him about earning medals. Because Bowker views the medals as meaningless, it is difficult for him to accept his father's admiration, which is based on the number of medals Bowker has won rather than his unquantifiable experience in the war.

O'Brien uses the images of the sewage field and the lake to illustrate the characters' inability to escape the effects of the Vietnam War. The sewage field is a vivid metaphor for an unpleasant, meaningless battle that none of the soldiers can escape. The sewage field's stench heightens the sensation that there is nothing valorous or heroic about this war; rather, it is debased and unclean. Bowker thinks that if it wasn't for the horrible smell he might have saved Kiowa and won the Silver Star. But just as Kiowa was unable to be saved from sinking into the field, Bowker cannot save himself from his repeated, almost obsessive thoughts about Kiowa and the Song Tra Bong. Likewise, his wading into the lake is a physical manifestation of his desire to return to that day in Vietnam and to change the course of events that ended in Kiowa's death in the muck.

"Notes"

> *By telling stories, you objectify your own experience. You separate it from yourself. You pin down certain truths. You make up others.* (See QUOTATIONS, p. 69)

Summary

O'Brien says that "Speaking of Courage" was written at the request of Norman Bowker who, three years after the story was written, hung himself in the YMCA. O'Brien says that in 1975, right before Saigon finally collapsed, he received a seventeen-page, handwritten letter from Bowker saying that he couldn't find a meaningful use for his life after the war. He worked several short-lived jobs and lived with his parents. At one point he enrolled in junior college, but he eventually dropped out.

In his letter, Bowker told O'Brien that he had read his first book, *If I Die in a Combat Zone,* and that the book had brought back a great deal of memories. Bowker then suggested that O'Brien write a story about someone who feels that Vietnam robbed him of his will to live—he said he would write it himself but he couldn't find the words. O'Brien explains that when he received Bowker's letter he thought about how easily he transitioned from Vietnam to graduate school at Harvard University. He thought that without writing, he himself might have been paralyzed.

While he was working on a new novel entitled *Going After Cacciato,* O'Brien thought of Bowker's suggestion and began a chapter titled "Speaking of Courage." But, following Bowker's request, he did not use Bowker's name. He substituted his own hometown scenery for Bowker's and he omitted the story of the sewage field and the rain and Kiowa's death in favor of his own protagonist's story. The writing was easy, and he published the piece as a separate short story. Later, O'Brien realized that the postwar piece had no place in *Going After Cacciato,* a war novel, and that in order to be successful, the story would have to stand on its own in truth, no matter how much the prospect frightened O'Brien. When the story was anthologized a year later, O'Brien sent a copy to Bowker, who was upset about the absence of Kiowa. Eight months later Bowker hung himself.

A decade later, O'Brien has revised the story and has come to terms with it—he says the central incident, about the night on the Song Tra Bong and the death of Kiowa, has been restored. But he contends that he does not want to imply that Bowker did *not* have a lapse of courage that was responsible for the death of Kiowa.

ANALYSIS

Although "Notes" is the second of three consecutive stories connected to Kiowa's death, it is more about O'Brien's own search for authenticity in storytelling than about the death itself. "Notes" is the only one of the three written in first person, which makes it the story closest to O'Brien's perspective. O'Brien focuses on the guilt that he feels not over Kiowa's death but over his own attempts to represent it inauthentically. His explanation that most of his writing comes from the "simple need to talk" illustrates that his writing is his chosen form of relief from mental anguish. As such, his success in dealing with his mental anguish is directly related to his success as a storyteller. Still, relief is not so easily earned. While O'Brien knows that telling Bowker's story will make easier his own grief-negotiation process, he struggles to find the appropriate venue to do so.

While "Speaking of Courage" introduces the postwar Norman Bowker and illustrates how the guilt he feels in regard to Kiowa's death follows him home to Iowa, "Notes" presents O'Brien's perspective on Bowker, enriched by the information that Bowker killed himself fewer than ten years after the war. In many ways, this story is a complement to "Speaking of Courage" as well as a sequel. The information provided in Bowker's letter allows us to understand how seriously he was affected by the war. Bowker's actions in "Speaking of Courage"—driving repeatedly around the lake, trying to strike up a conversation with the cashier at the A&W, wading in the lake with his clothes on—may seem incomprehensible, but the added information we gain from O'Brien's telling of the story illuminates why he acts as he does. Bowker's listlessness in the previous story is accounted for in the latter—his inability to find a method to communicate his feelings results in his suicide.

By working on this story and finessing it in order to make it accurately convey his feelings about Vietnam and specifically about Norman Bowker and Kiowa, O'Brien makes peace with his memories of them. He writes in order to remember in a way that is not painful. Therefore, though he originally leaves Kiowa's death out of "Speaking of Courage," he puts it back in because it is the essential part of understanding Bowker's despair and listlessness.

As in previous stories, O'Brien makes the boundaries between truth and fiction vague in order to suggest that telling a true war story is not contingent on any verifiable facts. For example, the chronology of the fictional O'Brien's writing career is quite similar to the real O'Brien's—*If I Die in a Combat Zone* and *Going After Cacciato* are names of novels that O'Brien the author actually published, and the mention of these real works raises the stakes for both the fictional O'Brien and for us. Reading "Speaking of Courage" takes on a new significance for us, for example, if a man named Norman Bowker actually killed himself. Also, Bowker's statement to O'Brien that he recognized himself among the characters of *If I Die in a Combat Zone* forges a closer link between O'Brien, who stands outside his works, and his characters, who inhabit them.

"In the Field"

Summary

The morning after Kiowa's death, the platoon wades in the mud of the sewage field with Jimmy Cross leading the way. Cross thinks of Kiowa and the crime that is his death. He concludes that although the order to camp came from a higher power, he made a mistake letting his men camp on the dangerous riverbank. He decides to write a letter to Kiowa's father saying what a good soldier Kiowa was.

When the search for Kiowa's body gets underway on the cold, wet morning, Azar begins cracking jokes about "eating shit" and "biting the dirt," and Bowker rebukes him. Halfway across the field, Mitchell Sanders discovers Kiowa's rucksack, and the men begin wading in the muck, desperately searching for the body.

Meanwhile, Jimmy Cross finishes composing the letter in his head and reflects that he never wanted the responsibility of leadership in the first place—he signed up for Reserve Officers Training Corps without giving thought to the consequences. He blames himself for making the wrong decision, concluding that he should have followed his first impulse and removed the men from the field. He feels that his oversight caused Kiowa's death. In the distance he notices the shaking body of a young soldier and goes over to speak to him. The soldier too blames himself for being unable to save Kiowa and becomes determined to find the body because Kiowa was carrying the only existing picture of the soldier's ex-girlfriend.

After the platoon has spent a half a day wading in the field, Azar ceases his joking. The men find Kiowa's body wedged between a layer of mud, take hold of the two boots, and pull. Unable to move it, they call over Dobbins and Kiley, who also help pull. After ten minutes and more pulling, Kiowa's body rises to the surface covered with blue-green mud. Harrowed and relieved, the men clean him up and then try to take their mind off him. Azar apologizes for the jokes.

Cross squats in the muck, revising the letter to Kiowa's father in his head. He notices the unnamed soldier, still searching for the missing picture. The soldier tries to get Cross's attention, saying he has to explain something. But Cross ignores him, choosing instead to float in the muck, thinking about blame, responsibility, and golf.

Analysis

"Speaking of Courage" gives Bowker's view of Kiowa's death, and "Notes" gives O'Brien's view. "In the Field" allows the other company members to comment. Like "Speaking of Courage," "In the Field" is told in the third person, but instead of focusing on one character's account of Kiowa's death, it gives many different points of view. We can relive the situation not only from Norman Bowker's point of view but also from that of Lieutenant Cross, Azar, and a young, unnamed soldier.

Through the character of Cross, "In the Field" addresses how a direct experience with death can change a person. Cross is not angry with the young soldier, who is more frustrated by the loss of his ex-girlfriend's picture than by the loss of his fellow soldier. However, Cross, more than most of the other soldiers, understands the power of pictures and tokens to elicit memories and keep thoughts away from war's atrocities. In "The Things They Carried," he feels his obsession with pictures of his unrequited beloved so distracting that he burns them all in a foxhole. In Cross's matter-of-fact response to Kiowa's death in "In the Field," O'Brien illustrates that war has shown Cross the importance of focusing on the task at hand rather than love far away. In times of war, O'Brien suggests, priorities become clear.

"In the Field" marks Azar's transformation from an immature soldier who mocks death into a sensitive comrade who feels the tragedy of death acutely. Azar's callousness and immaturity is illustrated once again in this story, but unlike in previous stories, here he actually sees the error of his ways and apologizes. Whereas before he uses his jokes and crassness as distancing tactics, now that he is forced to contend with Kiowa's body, buried deep in the muck, he feels guilty for his "wasted in the waste" comments. The sight of the actual body and the feeling of pulling it out of the earth that threatens to swallow it makes him feel guilty. Suddenly, death has been transported from the realm of the abstract and impossible into the realm of the concrete and probable. As an attempt to make himself feel better, he apologizes to the men who for so long have tried to shut him up. He finally feels the guilt and pain that the other men have been carrying with them about this incident and about Vietnam in general.

In spite of the gruesome images of death and the horrible task at hand for the company, this story, like several of the others, suggests that optimism cannot be quashed, even in the most tenuous of times.

At one point in the story, as the men are trying to unearth Kiowa's body, Henry Dobbins comments that things could be worse, suggesting an undefeatable hope against hope. Though Dobbins doesn't articulate how specifically things could be worse, the answer is implicit in the life-celebrating tone O'Brien uses in the rest of the story. The men feel giddy about being alive and being lucky, about being able to strip down and change clothes and start a fire. Each experience of death brings each man closer to life.

The guilt Jimmy Cross feels suggests that the weight of responsibility is debilitating for the inexperienced soldiers of Vietnam. We learn that Cross never wanted to be in charge of the men in the first place—he is only twenty-four years old, innocent, uninformed, and leading though his heart isn't in it. Sometimes he listens to instinct but other times, as in the case of setting up camp on the banks of the Song Tra Bong, he follows questionable advice from his superiors and later regrets it. Also, by this stage of the war, Cross understands that a part of taking responsibility is accepting blame. In the case of bad judgment, the blame is on him. Cross uses a technique for dealing with this burden of blame that is very similar to O'Brien's technique for dealing with survivor's guilt: he mentally composes a narrative. By writing a letter in his head to Kiowa's father and taking the responsibility for Kiowa's death, he successfully uses O'Brien's storytelling tactic to alleviate some of his feelings of guilt.

"Good Form"

Summary

O'Brien talks about the difference between real truth and story truth. He says he wants to explain the structure of his book. He says that he saw a man die on a trail near My Khe, but that he did not kill him. He then says that he made up this story. He says he wants us to feel what he felt and because of that, sometimes story truth is truer than happening truth. He says that what stories can do is make things present. Imagining Kathleen asking him if he's ever killed anyone, O'Brien envisions saying yes and then envisions saying no.

Analysis

O'Brien's willingness to contradict himself in this story illustrates the point that he is trying to make: it is not verifiable fact, but the validity of a story's sentiment that determines whether or not it is true. In "Good Form," the supposedly reliable narrator O'Brien says that he has made everything up, including the story about his killing a man outside My Khe, in order to throw off the reader. He then takes this tactic a step further by writing that even the contention that the stories are untrue could be an untrue statement. By attempting to alienate us in such a profound way, O'Brien provokes us to conclude that the largest truth in the telling of such stories is in the feelings instead of the facts. If, up until now, O'Brien's Vietnam stories have rung true, if they've seemed realistic and have made us identify with the plight of the characters, it shouldn't matter whether or not the facts are straight. In other words, since we experience, with O'Brien, how it feels to kill a man, it scarcely matters whether or not the killing occurred.

O'Brien's daughter Kathleen serves as O'Brien's model audience in "Good Form." She prompts him to consider the emotional truth of his stories and to juxtapose that truth with the disputed fact of whether or not he killed a man in My Khe. Kathleen's role as O'Brien's daughter raises the emotional stakes of the work as a whole. O'Brien wants to tell his story to her just as he wants to tell it to us, and his relationship to her mirrors his relationship to us.

"Field Trip"

Summary

O'Brien says that a few months after finishing the story "In the Field," he returns to the site of Kiowa's death with his daughter Kathleen and an intepreter. He says though the field does look familiar, it is not how he remembers it—everything, he says, is dry. Kathleen complains that the land stinks. She has just turned ten and has received the trip as a birthday gift intended to grant her insight into her father's history. But though she attempts to act tolerant, she is bored. She can't understand the war or why her father fought in it.

As she and O'Brien approach the field, Kathleen is amused by the interpreter's display of magic tricks. O'Brien reflects on the way the field, which now looks so different, could have the power to swallow his best friend and part of his life. He goes for a quick swim, surprising and disgusting Kathleen, who threatens to tell her mother. But before he leaves the river, he takes Kiowa's moccasins and leaves them in the spot where he imagines his friend settled into the river. When O'Brien returns, Kathleen asks him if an old man in the field is mad at him. O'Brien says that all the anger is finished.

Analysis

"Field Trip" explores the personal nature of memory and expands both the distance between us and O'Brien and that between O'Brien and Kathleen. When they travel to Vietnam, the thirty-four-year-old O'Brien and his ten-year-old daughter have profoundly different experiences interacting with the land. Kathleen complains, having no personal connection with the mucky water and the mysterious land. As a child, she cannot appreciate the area for what it is—a storehouse of memories for her father and an opportunity for him to come to terms with what happened so long ago and what has happened since. Most likely having a personal connection neither to O'Brien nor Vietnam, we, as readers, are put in Kathleen's predicament while reading *The Things They Carried*. Like Kathleen, we are shown the characters and the settings of Vietnam and are ourselves challenged to do what the immature Kathleen cannot—take in the history and allow a piece of it to affect us.

Although "Field Trip" addresses the sensitive issue of introducing the children of veterans to the war experience, the impracticality of O'Brien's attempt to share his experience with the young Kathleen quickly becomes clear. The title itself is a somewhat perverse and ironic pun: the field trip is, as the title implies, a childish lark, but it is also literally a trip to a field of war. These two levels of experience appear to be irreconcilable. Kathleen cannot be expected to understand the things that her father himself doesn't understand—especially since he hasn't even made a commitment to telling his daughter the whole truth. Furthermore, while O'Brien is interested in the truth that he can gain by comparing his memories to the reality of the significantly changed field, Kathleen is much more interested in the illusions and magic tricks their Vietnamese interpreter provides. Likewise, as O'Brien thinks that by swimming he is engaging in a profound act that honors the memory of Kiowa and relieves his own guilt, Kathleen sees her father's wading into the river as immature. In the space between father and daughter lies a silence that separates every storyteller from his or her audience.

In this story, O'Brien physically revisits a war experience in hopes of alleviating his guilt over Kiowa's death. Under the guise of a trip for his daughter, O'Brien comes to Vietnam to bury his guilt, bearing Kiowa's moccasins and wading into the muck to deposit them there. Like Bowker dousing himself in his Iowa lake on the Fourth of July, O'Brien attempts a ritual cleansing. Since the land looks so different, O'Brien feels a safe distance in the twenty years since the end of the war. The field is smaller and less menacing, perhaps because it is not in a state of war, perhaps because O'Brien is older, or perhaps, simply, because the land has changed with the passage of time. His response to Kathleen's question about whether an old farmer in the field is mad at them—that all the anger is finished—reveals not only his hope that he can conquer his past but also his need to do so.

"The Ghost Soldiers"

> *. . . after seven months in the bush I realized that those high, civilized trappings had somehow been crushed under the weight of the simple daily realities. I'd turned mean inside.*
>
> (See QUOTATIONS, p. 70)

Summary

O'Brien recalls that he was shot twice—the first time, images from Gene Autry movies race through his head, and he ends up on the lap of Rat Kiley, the medic. During and after his treatment, O'Brien appreciates Kiley's skill, courage, and ease. When O'Brien returns from his recovery almost a month later, Kiley has been wounded and shipped off and a new medic named Bobby Jorgenson has taken his place. When O'Brien is shot the second time, Jorgenson is incapable of treating his shock, and the result is a harrowing, painful experience for O'Brien.

The realization that he was near death for no good reason leaves O'Brien seething—he vows to exact revenge on the frightened, incompetent Jorgenson. He spends more time in the hospital and then is transferred to the battalion supply section, a far more comfortable and less dangerous assignment. Meanwhile, his backside hurts and he is forced to sleep on his stomach and smear antibacterial ointment on himself several times a day. During the miserable nights, he renews his vow to make Jorgenson pay.

When the company comes for a routine operation to where O'Brien is recovering, O'Brien meets the helicopters. He listens to stories from his friends—especially one about a soldier who decided to go for a swim and ended up with a disease that was later treated by Jorgenson—but he is most concerned with finding Jorgenson. Mitchell Sanders encourages O'Brien to leave Jorgenson alone, saying that he is one of the Alpha Company now and implying that O'Brien is no longer a member of the company. The next morning, O'Brien runs into Jorgenson, who apologizes for his inept treatment of O'Brien, saying that he was scared and that since O'Brien was shot, he has felt a great deal of remorse. O'Brien begins resenting Jorgenson for making him feel guilty.

O'Brien attempts to enlist his friends in his plans for revenge, but the only one who will concede to get involved is Azar. The two go to spook Jorgenson as he serves all-night duty. O'Brien says the amount of fear one feels multiplies as one sits alone, wondering and worrying. At midnight, they jerk some ropes, which gives the illusion of the enemy in the bush. O'Brien identifies with Jorgenson and feels his fear. Later, they set flares, and when Jorgenson bursts from his position and rolls toward a heap of sandbags, O'Brien finally feels vindicated. He tells Azar that he's had enough, but Azar, who loves to make trouble, wants to finish what they've started. O'Brien has a flashback of being shot, thinks about being in shock, and once again resents Jorgenson's deficiencies. He resolves to follow through.

Azar and O'Brien set off flare after flare and make a white sandbag move to spook Jorgenson further. But Jorgenson does not lose his cool—instead he advances toward O'Brien, calling out his name. Azar kicks O'Brien in the head, declares him pathetic, and goes off to bed. He later reconciles with O'Brien. The two men shake hands, and Jorgenson compliments O'Brien's dramatic touch and asks him if they're even now. The two jokingly decide to scare Azar.

Analysis

Like Curt Lemon and Rat Kiley, O'Brien has wartime fears that are sometimes more acute than the actual pain of war itself. O'Brien speaks in specific terms about getting shot—he leads us through the experience and makes it real for us—in order to illustrate that despite the movies and war legends, the pain of being shot is a survivable pain. Like Curt Lemon, whose fear of pain finds him provoking a dentist into pulling his tooth, O'Brien realizes that the actual pain surrounding a wound is nowhere near as frightening as grappling with the notion of being shot.

O'Brien's second experience being shot reveals the extent of his disillusionment. This time, the novelty of the situation has worn off, and what remains is frustration, anguish, and anger at Bobby Jorgenson who, neither qualified nor certain, does not help O'Brien the way he wants to be helped. As a result, O'Brien's second experience being wounded doesn't need the mantra or the movie images—it is all too real, as he falls into shock and later almost dies of gangrene. Despite time and healing, he can't forgive the wrong he feels Jorgenson's ineptness has done him. When he finally gets the opportunity, he feels only the desire for cold, vicious, unmerciful revenge.

"Ghost Soldiers" demonstrates the tension between a soldier's need for camaraderie and the difficulty of finding it. O'Brien's anger can at least partially be traced to his newfound alienation. After he is wounded the second time he is stationed near the rear of "Headquarters Company" in a much safer and more comfortable company. But instead of the relief that we think he might feel as a result of being in a safer place, O'Brien is upset about missing the adventure of combat. When his company visits, he is no longer part of the group. For the first time, he is the listener of war stories instead of the teller. Creeping up on him, perhaps stirring up the evil feelings and desire for revenge, are feelings of alienation, nostalgia, and envy.

"Ghost Soldiers" recounts a progression in O'Brien's perspective from prewar idealism to postwar disillusionment. In "On the Rainy River," O'Brien, innocent and untouched by pain, feels obligation to people and a driving need to do the right thing. By the time of "Ghost Soldiers," however, the cruel, inexplicable ambiguity of war has clouded O'Brien's worldview. He not only feels no obligation to other people, he feels an intense need for unfounded revenge. After being mistreated by Jorgenson, O'Brien finds a new evil lying within him—an absolute desire to inflict pain on another human being and fellow soldier. Like Mary Anne Bell in "Sweetheart of the Song Tra Bong," O'Brien finds an inner truth as he feels anger and yearns for revenge. Against his better judgment, his good grooming, and his rational thinking, he is forced to hurt in order to avenge hurt.

"Night Life"

Summary

Although O'Brien isn't there when Rat Kiley sustains the injury that gets him sent to Japan, Mitchell Sanders relays the story later. When the platoon is in the foothills west of Quang Ngai City, they receive word of possible danger, so they sleep all day and march all night. The tension affects the men in different ways—Jensen takes vitamins, Cross takes NoDoz, and Kiley simply retreats into himself. For six days he says nothing, and then he can't stop talking. He begins scratching himself constantly and complaining of the bugs. It is sad, Sanders later remembers, and strange, but everyone feels the effects of the operation. They are chasing ghosts. One afternoon, Kiley almost breaks down, confessing to Sanders that he doesn't think he is cut out to be a medic, always picking up parts and plugging up holes. He mentions Ted Lavender and Curt Lemon, incredulous that they could be so alive one moment and so dead the next. He says that he is haunted by images of body parts, especially at night. He sees his own body and he imagines bugs chewing through him. The next morning, he shoots himself in the toe—an injury large enough to earn his release from duty. No one blames him, and Cross, the biggest critic of Kiley's cowardice, says that he will vouch for him.

Analysis

"Night Life" pits the drive for survival against the desire for social acceptance. O'Brien mentions that though most soldiers knew it was an option, they did not deliberately shoot themselves in the foot, out of a sense of shame, since shooting oneself would be an act of cowardice. "Night Life" both supports and refutes O'Brien's contention that men are too afraid of shame to leave the kill-or-be-killed life of war. Like Curt Lemon in "The Dentist," Kiley is less afraid of abject and unnecessary physical pain than he is of the unknown. This fear drives him to risk showing his cowardice—his fellow soldiers know that his wound is self-inflicted, and they know that fear drove him to do it. In the end, Kiley decides to give himself a minor wound instead of facing the decision of killing or being killed.

The Alpha Company's reaction to Kiley's shooting himself in the foot is consistent with its reaction to death: to these men, refusal to serve is as undesirable as death itself. Instead of addressing the situation, whether or not they agree with Kiley's action, they use a similar tactic to the one they use to confront death—they begin thinking and talking of something else, something completely unrelated. They dwell on the night life in Japan for the same reason Cross carries the picture of his unrequited love and Dobbins carries his girlfriend's stockings around his neck—women lie in a realm of comfort and distraction far away from the horrors of the war.

Kiley's breakdown is both shunned and desired by the other soldiers. Only because Kiley is so close to the edge can he, in the end, let himself go, openly lament the loss of his friends, and scream in incredulity about the unfairness of the war. Kiley's breakdown to Mitchell Sanders, which includes references to the deaths of Ted Lavender and Curt Lemon, makes more clear the others' simultaneous scorn and envy. Of course the soldiers must realize how close each has come to this same breaking point. In this way, they live vicariously through Kiley as they wave him goodbye. For they are at least a bit jealous: unlike O'Brien, whose fear of embarrassment delivers him to Vietnam in the first place, Rat Kiley, in the end, is willing to take the cetain shame for relief from the harrowing experiences of war.

"THE LIVES OF THE DEAD"

> *... when I take a high leap into the dark and come down thirty years later, I realize it is as Tim trying to save Timmy's life with a story.* (See QUOTATIONS, p. 71)

SUMMARY

O'Brien has been at war for only four days when the platoon is fired on by a village near the South China Sea. Cross orders an air strike and the platoon watches the village burn. Dave Jensen pokes fun at a dead old man whose right arm has been blown off and encourages O'Brien to do the same, to "show a little respect for your elders." O'Brien refuses, and Kiowa tells him he's done the right thing. He asks if the old man was O'Brien's first experience with a dead body, and O'Brien says no, thinking of his first date, Linda.

During the spring of 1956, O'Brien was in love with nine-year-old Linda, his beautifully fragile schoolmate who had taken to wearing a red cap everywhere. He arranged for his parents to take him and Linda to the movies, to see *The Man Who Never Was*—a World War II film that contained an image of a corpse falling into the sea. When the movie was over, and the two couples had made a stop at Dairy Queen, they dropped Linda off, and the fourth-grade O'Brien knew then that he was in love.

Linda continued to wear her red cap every day, despite being taunted for it. One day a fellow classmate, Nick Veenhof, pulled off the cap, revealing Linda's slowly balding head. Linda said nothing. O'Brien later explains that Linda had a brain tumor and soon died. He had known she was sick, but Nick was the one to break the news, saying O'Brien's girlfriend had "kicked the bucket." O'Brien went to the funeral home with his father and marveled at how strange and unreal it was to see Linda's body in a casket. He stared for a while, saying nothing, until his father, unable to address the situation, proposed a trip to the ice cream store. Later, O'Brien became withdrawn and obsessed with falling asleep. In daydreams and night dreams, he could make up stories about Linda, imagine her, and bring her back to life. In those dreams, Linda comforted O'Brien, telling him that it didn't matter that she was dead.

O'Brien says that in Vietnam, the soldiers devised ways to make the dead seem less dead—they kept them alive with stories, such as the stories of Ted Lavender's tranquilizer use or Curt Lemon's trick-or-treating. O'Brien remembers that he saw Linda's body in the funeral home, but that it upset him because it didn't seem real. He says that he picked Curt Lemon out of a tree and watched Kiowa sink into the muck of the Song Tra Bong, but that he still dreamed Linda alive in stories and in dreams. In his dreams, when he was young, Linda waited for him and stayed alive, if just sometimes obscured by other things happening. In stories, O'Brien concludes, the dead live.

Analysis

Though the work's final statement seems to have little to do with Vietnam, its relevance lies in its addressing of the intimate relationship between death and life. O'Brien uses "The Lives of the Dead" to illustrate that his war narrative has a larger purpose than simply showing readers what it was like to be in a war. Interspersed throughout this story are smaller stories about death in Vietnam that lead back to the story of O'Brien himself—a man who writes in order to make sense of his life, especially in relation to others' deaths. But at the forefront is the story of O'Brien's first love and of his first realization that fiction can overcome death.

The character of Linda, for the narrator, is synonymous with his loss of innocence. With her, he experiences both love and death for the first time, at the same time. In the story, she first represents the promise of childhood—delicate and beautiful, she agrees to go with him and his parents to the movies. When her balding head is revealed, and later her corpse, Linda's innocence—and O'Brien's, by association—is lost forever.

Linda's death is more profound than the tragedy of the deaths of Ted Lavender, Curt Lemon, and Kiowa. Unlike the soldiers, Linda, innocent, did nothing to provoke the dangers she faced. But once death's omnipresence and inevitability became clear, first to Linda, and later, when it was too late, to O'Brien, her death became an inevitability and sadness a negotiable feeling for him.

The way O'Brien looks at Linda's body in the funeral home and then thinks with detachment that it looks different than he thought it would becomes O'Brien's method for dealing with death for the rest of his life. Though he is so struck, he doesn't want to talk about it to his father, who, like his future comrades, tries to distract O'Brien rather than address his son's thoughts about death. O'Brien's subconscious then takes charge of helping O'Brien cope with his loss, as Linda begins to visit his dreams and teaches him to address the difficult and unknown through his imagination. Instead of frightening him, her specter brings comfort. The young O'Brien came to enjoy having the ability to talk to Linda so much that he looked forward to going to sleep, finding a comfort in the unreal that the real could no longer offer.

The end of *The Things They Carried* shows how the illusion of life that O'Brien uses to sustain him through Linda's death helps him in Vietnam and especially afterward. He compares his own coping strategy of storytelling to the crass coping strategies of the other men, who shake hands with corpses and joke about cleaning up the remains of their friends. Nevertheless, he realizes that these actions do help others deal with death, so he does not condemn his fellow soldiers. While the other soldiers joke or keep silent in regard to Ted Lavender and Curt Lemon, for example, O'Brien remembers their qualities and keeps them alive through the stories of the way they were when they were alive. O'Brien's confession that even though he is forty-three years old he is still making up stories that keep Linda alive reveals that these stories help keep him alive as well. O'Brien's worldview is one of acceptance and peace in the face of death, of celebrating the dead by remembering them living. The effect of O'Brien's seemingly arbitrary step into his distant past makes his war stories not only love stories, but life stories as well.

Important Quotations Explained

1. They carried the soldier's greatest fear, which was the fear of blushing. Men killed, and died, because they were embarrassed not to. It was what had brought them to the war in the first place, nothing positive, no dreams of glory or honor, just to avoid the blush of dishonor. They died so as not to die of embarrassment.

This quotation from the first story, "The Things They Carried," is part of a longer passage about the emotional baggage of men at risk of dying. O'Brien contends that barely restrained cowardice is a common secret among soldiers. He debunks the notion that men go to war to be heroes. Instead, he says, they go because they are forced to and because refusal equals cowardice. This detached generalization foreshadows several later references to courage and juxtapositions of courage and cowardice. In "On The Rainy River," O'Brien explains that the only thing that kept him from listening to his own convictions and running away from the war and across the border to Canada was the notion that the people in his hometown would think him a coward. Later, O'Brien kills a man himself and is forced to negotiate his guilt with his fellow soldiers' rationalization that killing was the right thing to do. By alluding to this killing early, and indicating that men do unspeakable things partly because of impulse but mostly because of peer pressure, O'Brien suggests that the greatest fear of all soldiers is not death or killing but simple embarrassment. By pinning the unnecessary deaths of his friends, especially Kiowa, on these false notions of obligation, O'Brien suggests that the greatest tragedy of the Vietnam War is not its violence but its ability to inspire compliance.

2. He was a slim, dead, almost dainty young man of about twenty. He lay with one leg bent beneath him, his jaw in his throat, his face neither expressive nor inexpressive. One eye was shut. The other was a star-shaped hole.

This quotation, from "The Man I Killed," describes the corpse of a young Vietnamese soldier whom O'Brien killed with a grenade. In this story, the narration is from a third-person perspective, and is largely a series of unconnected observations and fantasies about the young, dead soldier. This particular passage is an example of the concrete description O'Brien uses to come to terms with his killing of the boy. He is blunt in these moments, perhaps because he thinks matter-of-factness is the only way to negotiate committing the unthinkable. But the observation that the man is dainty and the idea that his face might hold an expression speak to the humanity of both the dead young man and that of his killer-turned-observer. O'Brien's description of the star-shaped hole in the boy's eye is both a means of detaching himself and an idea that in death a body becomes mystical and beautiful. These particular words become a refrain for O'Brien—they are repeated several times in reference to this killing, to reinforce the notion that the memory of the young man's body is one still fresh in O'Brien's mind.

3. By telling stories, you objectify your own experience. You separate it from yourself. You pin down certain truths. You make up others. You start sometimes with an incident that truly happened, like the night in the shit field, and you carry it forward by inventing incidents that did not in fact occur but that nonetheless help to clarify and explain.

This passage comes from "Notes," a story about O'Brien's efforts to allay Norman Bowker's guilt about Kiowa's death and his feelings of aimlessness after the war by telling a story. O'Brien reflects on his own storytelling after Bowker sends him a letter asking for a story because he, Bowker, wants to explain his feelings of frustration and disillusionment but doesn't know what to say. The letter inspires O'Brien to consider his own storytelling as a means for coping with his traumatic experiences. This particular passage is one of several that support O'Brien's contention that in storytelling, objective truth is not as important as the feeling that a story gives. Later, in "Good Form," O'Brien says that the stories he tells may be entirely made up and forces us to decide whether his characters and contentions are just as powerful and valid if the facts behind them are simply made up. All of this commentary serves to prove that sometimes, in storytelling, factual truth is not as important as emotional truth.

4. I'd come to this war a quiet, thoughtful sort of person, a college grad, Phi Beta Kappa and summa cum laude, all the credentials, but after seven months in the bush I realized that those high, civilized trappings had somehow been crushed under the weight of the simple daily realities. I'd turned mean inside.

When, in "The Ghost Soldiers," O'Brien tries to exact revenge on Bobby Jorgensen for his failure to treat him competently, he concedes that he is acting irrationally. Though it is difficult for O'Brien to admit, after a certain amount of time in Vietnam he realizes that he is capable of evil. The only way for him to deal with hurt is to hurt back. The terms O'Brien uses juxtapose his previous life—one of intellectualism and striving for success through studying—with his life in the jungle, where accolades like Phi Beta Kappa have no relevance. The foreign, academic terms "Phi Beta Kappa" and "summa cum laude" contrast starkly with the simple, blunt descriptions of life in the "bush," just as the civility of his college years contrasts starkly with his newfound meanness.

5. [S]ometimes I can even see Timmy skating with Linda under the yellow floodlights. I'm young and happy. I'll never die. I'm skimming across the surface of my own history, moving fast, riding the melt beneath the blades, doing loops and spins, and when I take a high leap into the dark and come down thirty years later, I realize it is as Tim trying to save Timmy's life with a story.

In the closing story, "The Lives of the Dead," O'Brien broadens the scope of his work by juxtaposing his first encounter with death as a soldier with his first-ever experience with death when, at age nine, his friend Linda succumbed to a brain tumor. In this particular passage, O'Brien explains how memory and storytelling are comforts for times of mourning and how they have equipped him to deal with the painful past. In this extended metaphor, he considers how his need to tell stories evolved through daydreams of Linda. He is optimistic that the power of memory in storytelling gives immortality to both the one who has died—in this case Linda, making her vibrant and able to skate with Timmy in a warmly lit dream—and the one who tells the story—in this case O'Brien, enabling O'Brien to cope with his traumatic past.

Key Facts

FULL TITLE
The Things They Carried

AUTHOR
Tim O'Brien

TYPE OF WORK
Collection of interconnected short stories

GENRE
War stories; coming-of-age stories; memory stories

LANGUAGE
English

TIME AND PLACE WRITTEN
Massachusetts, late 1980s

DATE OF FIRST PUBLICATION
1990

PUBLISHER
Houghton Mifflin / Seymour Lawrence

NARRATOR
Tim O'Brien

POINT OF VIEW
Most of the stories are told from the first person, but on several occasions, O'Brien uses the third person as either a distancing tactic or a chance to let one of his platoon-mates, such as Mitchell Sanders or Rat Kiley, tell his story.

TONE
The Things They Carried is an introspective memory story and a self-conscious examination of the methods and reasons behind storytelling. The narrator is unreliable; he speaks of the necessity of blurring truth and fiction in a true war story.

TENSE
Past tense, shifting between the Vietnam War in the late 1960s and the narrator's immediate past, twenty years after the war

SETTING (TIME)
Late 1960s and late 1980s

SETTING (PLACE)
Vietnam and Massachusetts

PROTAGONIST
Tim O'Brien

MAJOR CONFLICT
The men of the Alpha Company, especially Tim O'Brien, grapple with the effects—both immediate and long-term—of the Vietnam War.

RISING ACTION
In the summer of 1968, Tim O'Brien receives a draft notice. Despite a desire to follow his convictions and flee to Canada, he feels he would be embarrassed to refuse to fulfill his patriotic duty and so concedes to fight in Vietnam.

CLIMAX
During their tour of duty, the men of the Alpha Company must cope with the loss of their own men and the guilt that comes from killing and watching others die.

FALLING ACTION
After he returns from war, O'Brien grapples with his memories by telling stories about Vietnam.

THEMES
Physical and emotional burdens; fear of shame as motivaton; the subjection of truth to storytelling

MOTIFS
Storytelling; ambiguous morality; loneliness and isolation

SYMBOLS
The dead young Vietnamese soldier; Kathleen; Linda

FORESHADOWING
O'Brien mentions the deaths of men such as Ted Lavender, Curt Lemon, and Kiowa before he gives detailed accounts of how and when they died in later stories.

Study Questions & Essay Topics

Study Questions

1. *Discuss the idea of carrying in O'Brien's work. What things are carried, and by whom?*

The theme of carrying is an important one throughout the text, and the title story provides the most comprehensive examination of this idea. The dense and detailed lists of objects that the men carry may seem tedious or irrelevant at times, but by mentioning that in addition to weapons soldiers brought mundane things like candy, cigarettes, and letters from their loved ones, O'Brien emphasizes their humanity. And in specifying the exact weight of several of the items, including food, weapons, and gear, he gives us a very tangible idea of what it was like to struggle under such weight.

But the soldiers carry more than just physical burdens—in many cases, they are weighed down by emotional baggage. Jimmy Cross thinks that he carried the idea of Martha so heavily, for example, that he caused Ted Lavender's death. And because Ted Lavender carries so much anxiety—and tranquilizers and marijuana to slow him down and soothe him—he may not be paying attention while walking around, resulting in his being shot.

The metaphor of carrying is important to O'Brien's work as a whole and extends through the different stories in order to give weight to the idea that the things one carries—whether physical or emotional—enable us to navigate life's inconsistencies. Many of the characters and items introduced in the first story are carried by O'Brien into the later stories. Kiowa's Bible and the effect it has on his life is a major topic of conversation in "Church." Henry Dobbins's character can be explained by the fact that he carries his girlfriend's pantyhose around his neck, and in "Stockings," O'Brien recounts what happens after the girlfriend breaks up with Dobbins. These recurring details indicate that personalities remained constant in Vietnam and that the beliefs and hopes of the main characters sustained these personalities throughout their time in the war.

2. *Discuss the use of third-person narration in the work. Since most of the work is personal and written from a first-person perspective, what purpose does third-person narration serve? Why is the collection's title phrased in the third-person plural?*

In telling stories, O'Brien is able to gain some distance from the harrowing experience he had in Vietnam. Several of the stories in the work, specifically those centered on a particularly painful experience, are told from a third-person point of view, so that O'Brien can sustain a distance from his memories. For example, in "The Man I Killed," O'Brien describes the physical characteristics of the Vietnamese soldier's corpse and illustrates how his fellow soldiers react to his killing the man, but he doesn't at any point describe how he feels about the situation. His guilt is implicit in this lack of response. Like the other men of the Alpha Company, who would rather joke about how their comrades' corpses look than deal with the impact of death, O'Brien uses third-person narration to achieve a distance that would have been impossible with first-person narration.

The use of the third person also gives a certain amount of universality to the work—indeed, O'Brien doesn't think that his experience is any more horrific than that of his fellow soldiers. He realizes, for example, that he was not the only soldier to experience Kiowa's death, and that Norman Bowker and Jimmy Cross experienced it differently and just as validly. The work is titled *The Things They Carried,* rather than *The Things I Carried,* because O'Brien is not speaking simply for himself, or even for his company of soldiers. As is evident from the change of subject in the last story—to the death of Linda, O'Brien's first love—O'Brien is not even speaking only about Vietnam. The idea that people carry heavy emotional burdens is a universal one, and the alternation between first-person narrative and third-person narrative is a reflection of O'Brien's belief that by telling his own story, he is telling the story of many.

3. *What is the role of women in* The Things They Carried?

Although women play a small role in *The Things They Carried,* it is a significant one. Female characters such as Martha, Mary Anne Bell, and Henry Dobbins's unnamed girlfriend all affect the men of the Alpha Company—although in two of the cases, the women aren't even with the men they're affecting. The men idealize the women and use their presence—in letters, photographs, and even their imagination—as a kind of solace and reminder that a world does exist outside the atrocities of Vietnam. Jimmy Cross, for example, carries pictures of Martha and memories of their only date. He carries, also, the hope that she might one day return his love so that he has something to look forward to, after the war. Henry Dobbins carries his girlfriend's pantyhose for a similar reason: to remind him of home and to distract him from the harsh realities of being the machine gunner in a platoon of soldiers. Mark Fossie invites his girlfriend Mary Anne over to Vietnam because he believes her presence might save him from the horrors before him. These men do not think of these women as beings with thoughts, fears, and needs. They instead see them as motivation to survive the war.

But the women in *The Things They Carried* don't always fulfill the fantasy role that the men carve out for them. We learn in "Love" that even after Jimmy Cross returns home from the war, he cannot ever win Martha's heart. Similarly, after a short while in Vietnam, Mary Anne Bell falls captive to the jungle's mystery and ends up leaving Mark Fossie and breaking his heart. Sometimes, in the end, though, the reality is not enough to affect the man holding a female fantasy—even after Henry Dobbins's girlfriend breaks up with him, he still believes her pantyhose will bring him good luck.

Suggested Essay Topics

1. "The Man I Killed" is the only story that focuses primarily on a Vietnamese character. Why does this shift in focus occur in this particular story? Why are Vietnamese characters largely absent from the rest of the text?

2. Although the work is supposedly about the Vietnam war, the final story focuses not on the war but on an episode from O'Brien's childhood. Discuss how this story relates to the stories of the war. What is O'Brien's purpose in ending his collection of stories this way?

3. What do the terms "story-truth" and "happening-truth" mean in the context of the book? How do they differ?

4. Although *The Things They Carried* contains a story called "The Man I Killed," it is unclear whether O'Brien actually killed anyone in Vietnam. What purpose does this ambiguity serve?

5. How does shame fit into O'Brien's portrayal of the war experience?

6. Discuss the structure of the work. Do the stories progress in a linear manner? How does the work's fragmented style contribute to the themes that run through the stories?

Review & Resources

Quiz

1. What kind of gun does Henry Dobbins carry?

    A. M-60B
    B. M-14
    C. M-16
    D. M-79

2. What is Jimmy Cross's rank?

    A. Private
    B. Colonel
    C. Lieutenant
    D. Medic

3. What sport did Martha play at Mount Sebastian College?

    A. Tennis
    B. Soccer
    C. Field hockey
    D. Volleyball

4. Why does Ted Lavender take tranquilizers?

    A. His leg was blown off by a mine
    B. Dave Jensen broke his nose
    C. He is generally nervous
    D. Someone sent them to him as a gift

5. How does Ted Lavender die?

    A. A grenade he's playing catch with explodes
    B. He is shot in the head
    C. He steps on a mortar round
    D. He catches a disease swimming in a river

6. How do Jimmy Cross and Martha reunite?

    A. At a college reunion
    B. They never speak to one another again
    C. They marry after the war
    D. They serve as missionaries in several third-world countries

7. What is the average age of the Alpha Company members?

    A. 30–35
    B. 28–30
    C. 19–20
    D. 22–25

8. What is O'Brien's summer job before the war?

    A. He works on a political campaign
    B. He works at the Tip Top Lodge
    C. He works in a meatpacking factory
    D. He works on a draft board

9. What is the outcome of the fight between Dave Jensen and Lee Strunk over Jensen's missing jackknife?

    A. Jensen breaks Strunk's nose
    B. Strunk blows Jensen's leg off
    C. Strunk gives back Jensen's jackknife
    D. Jimmy Cross breaks up the fight

10. What is the pact between Jensen and Strunk?

    A. They will play a trick on Azar when he is on night watch
    B. They will each try to kill a Vietnamese soldier
    C. If one gets badly injured, the other will make sure he dies
    D. Neither of them will say who really stole the jackknife

11. How is Curt Lemon killed?

   A. He is shot in the head
   B. He steps on a mine
   C. He is never killed
   D. He plays catch with a grenade that goes off

12. What happens when Curt Lemon is called in to see the dentist?

   A. Lemon faints
   B. The dentist finds a cavity
   C. Lemon runs away and refuses to go
   D. Lemon knocks out one of the dentist's teeth

13. Who flies his girlfriend to Vietnam?

   A. Tim O'Brien
   B. Mark Fossie
   C. Mitchell Sanders
   D. Henry Dobbins

14. At the end of "Sweetheart of the Song Tra Bong," what is Mary Anne Bell wearing?

   A. A flak jacket
   B. An army helmet
   C. The skin of a Vietnamese casualty
   D. A necklace of tongues

15. Who tells the story of "Sweetheart of the Song Tra Bong"?

   A. Rat Kiley
   B. Tim O'Brien
   C. Mitchell Sanders
   D. Mark Fossie

16. What item does Henry Dobbins wear around his neck?

   A. Dog tags
   B. Ammunition
   C. A locket from his girlfriend
   D. His girlfriend's pantyhose

17. How does O'Brien kill a Vietnamese soldier outside My Khe?

    A. He wrestles him to the ground and stabs him
    B. He shoots him point-blank
    C. He tosses a grenade at his feet
    D. He drowns him in a well

18. When the platoon burns a village and then finds a young girl dancing, who mocks her?

    A. Rat Kiley
    B. Norman Bowker
    C. Tim O'Brien
    D. Azar

19. What medal does Norman Bowker almost win?

    A. The Air Medal
    B. The Silver Star
    C. The Bronze Star
    D. The Purple Heart

20. Where does Kiowa die?

    A. In a helicopter on its way to Japan
    B. In a pagoda that gets hit by a bomb
    C. In the muck near the Song Tra Bong
    D. On the way to My Khe

21. Who runs the Tip Top Lodge?

    A. Jimmy Cross
    B. Elroy Berdahl
    C. Norman Bowker
    D. Tim O'Brien

22. What does a young soldier share with Kiowa the night before Kiowa's death?

    A. A picture of his girlfriend
    B. A joint
    C. Three-month old Christmas cookies
    D. His copy of the New Testament

23. When O'Brien returns to Vietnam more than twenty years after the war, whom does he bring with him?

    A. His wife
    B. Mary Anne Bell
    C. Kathleen
    D. Norman Bowker

24. A few days after O'Brien arrives in Vietnam, who tells him to "introduce himself" to a corpse?

    A. Azar
    B. Dave Jensen
    C. Norman Bowker
    D. Kiowa

25. Why did O'Brien's relationship with Linda end?

    A. She left him for another man
    B. He had to leave for Vietnam
    C. She ran off into the wilderness, never to be heard from again
    D. She died of a brain tumor

Answer Key:
1: A; 2: C; 3: D; 4: C; 5: B; 6: A; 7: C; 8: C; 9: A; 10: C; 11: B; 12: A; 13: B; 14: D; 15: A; 16: D; 17: C; 18: D; 19: B; 20: C; 21: B; 22: A; 23: C; 24: B; 25: D

SUGGESTIONS FOR FURTHER READING

BATES, MILTON J. "Men, Women, and Vietnam." *America Rediscovered: Critical Essays on the Literature and Film of the Vietnam War.* Eds. Owen Gilman Jr. and Lorrie Smith, 27–63. New York: Garland, 1990.

BEIDLER, PHILIP D. *American Literature and the Experience of Vietnam.* Athens, Georgia: University of Georgia Press, 1982.

CALLOWAY, CATHERINE. "'How to Tell a True War Story': Metafiction in *The Things They Carried.*" *Critique* 36 (Summer 1995): 249–257.

HELLMAN, JOHN. *American Myth and the Legacy of Vietnam.* New York: Columbia University Press, 1986.

HERZOG, TOBEY C. *Tim O'Brien.* New York: Simon and Schuster Macmillan, 1997.

KAPLAN, STEVEN. *Understanding Tim O'Brien.* Columbia: University of South Carolina Press, 1995.

MELLING, PHILIP H. *Vietnam in American Literature.* Boston: Twayne Publishers, 1990.

O'BRIEN, TIM. "The Vietnam in Me." *New York Times Magazine,* October 2, 1994.

TEGMARK, MATS. *In the Shoes of a Soldier: Communication in Tim O'Brien's Vietnam Narratives.* Sweden: Uppsala, 1998.

SPARKNOTES TEST PREPARATION GUIDES

The SparkNotes team figured it was time to cut standardized tests down to size. We've studied the tests for you, so that SparkNotes test prep guides are:

Smarter:
Packed with critical-thinking skills and test-
  taking strategies that will improve your score.

Better:
Fully up to date, covering all new features of the tests,
  with study tips on every type of question.

Faster:
Our books cover exactly what you need to
  know for the test. No more, no less.

SparkNotes Guide to the SAT & PSAT
SparkNotes Guide to the SAT & PSAT—Deluxe Internet Edition
SparkNotes Guide to the ACT
SparkNotes Guide to the ACT—Deluxe Internet Edition
SparkNotes Guide to the SAT II Writing
SparkNotes Guide to the SAT II U.S. History
SparkNotes Guide to the SAT II Math Ic
SparkNotes Guide to the SAT II Math IIc
SparkNotes Guide to the SAT II Biology
SparkNotes Guide to the SAT II Physics

SAT and PSAT are registered trademarks of the College Entrance Examination Board, which does not endorse these books.
ACT is a registered trademark of ACT, Inc. which neither sponsors nor endorses these books.

SparkNotes Study Guides:

- 1984
- The Adventures of Huckleberry Finn
- The Adventures of Tom Sawyer
- The Aeneid
- All Quiet on the Western Front
- And Then There Were None
- Angela's Ashes
- Animal Farm
- Anne of Green Gables
- Anthem
- Antony and Cleopatra
- As I Lay Dying
- As You Like It
- The Awakening
- The Bean Trees
- The Bell Jar
- Beloved
- Beowulf
- Billy Budd
- Black Boy
- Bless Me, Ultima
- The Bluest Eye
- Brave New World
- The Brothers Karamazov
- The Call of the Wild
- Candide
- The Canterbury Tales
- Catch-22
- The Catcher in the Rye
- The Chosen
- Cold Mountain
- Cold Sassy Tree
- The Color Purple
- The Count of Monte Cristo
- Crime and Punishment
- The Crucible
- Cry, the Beloved Country
- Cyrano de Bergerac
- David Copperfield
- Death of a Salesman
- The Diary of a Young Girl
- Doctor Faustus
- A Doll's House
- Don Quixote
- Dr. Jekyll and Mr. Hyde
- Dracula
- Dune
- Emma
- Ethan Frome
- Fahrenheit 451
- Fallen Angels
- A Farewell to Arms
- Flowers for Algernon
- The Fountainhead
- Frankenstein
- The Glass Menagerie
- Gone With the Wind
- The Good Earth
- The Grapes of Wrath
- Great Expectations
- The Great Gatsby
- Grendel
- Gulliver's Travels
- Hamlet
- The Handmaid's Tale
- Hard Times
- Harry Potter and the Sorcerer's Stone
- Heart of Darkness
- Henry IV, Part I
- Henry V
- Hiroshima
- The Hobbit
- The House of the Seven Gables
- I Know Why the Caged Bird Sings
- The Iliad
- Inferno
- Invisible Man
- Jane Eyre
- Johnny Tremain
- The Joy Luck Club
- Julius Caesar
- The Jungle
- The Killer Angels
- King Lear
- The Last of the Mohicans
- Les Misérables
- A Lesson Before Dying
- The Little Prince
- Little Women
- Lord of the Flies
- The Lord of the Rings
- Macbeth
- Madame Bovary
- A Man for All Seasons
- The Mayor of Casterbridge
- The Merchant of Venice
- A Midsummer Night's Dream
- Moby-Dick
- Much Ado About Nothing
- My Ántonia
- Mythology
- Narrative of the Life of Frederick Douglass
- Native Son
- The New Testament
- Night
- Notes from Underground
- The Odyssey
- The Oedipus Trilogy
- Of Mice and Men
- The Old Man and the Sea
- The Old Testament
- Oliver Twist
- The Once and Future King
- One Flew Over the Cuckoo's Nest
- One Hundred Years of Solitude
- Othello
- Our Town
- The Outsiders
- Paradise Lost
- A Passage to India
- The Pearl
- The Picture of Dorian Gray
- Poe's Short Stories
- A Portrait of the Artist as a Young Man
- Pride and Prejudice
- The Prince
- A Raisin in the Sun
- The Red Badge of Courage
- The Republic
- Richard III
- Robinson Crusoe
- Romeo and Juliet
- The Scarlet Letter
- A Separate Peace
- Silas Marner
- Sir Gawain and the Green Knight
- Slaughterhouse-Five
- Snow Falling on Cedars
- Song of Solomon
- The Sound and the Fury
- Steppenwolf
- The Stranger
- A Streetcar Named Desire
- The Sun Also Rises
- A Tale of Two Cities
- The Taming of the Shrew
- The Tempest
- Tess of the d'Urbervilles
- Their Eyes Were Watching God
- Things Fall Apart
- The Things They Carried
- To Kill a Mockingbird
- To the Lighthouse
- Treasure Island
- Twelfth Night
- Ulysses
- Uncle Tom's Cabin
- Walden
- War and Peace
- Wuthering Heights
- A Yellow Raft in Blue Water